BROKEN

BLACKWATER PACK #1.5

HANNAH MCBRIDE

*Ali –
Break the cycle!
♡
Hannah McB*

Copyright © 2020 by Hannah McBride

BROKEN

Blackwater Pack Series, Book 1.5

Original Publication Date: October 30, 2020

ALL RIGHTS RESERVED. This book contains material protected under International and Federal Copyright Laws and Treaties. Any unauthorized reprint or use of this material is prohibited. No part of this book may be reproduced or transmitted in any form or by any means, electronic or mechanical, including photocopying, recording, or by an information and retrieval system without express written permission from the Author/Publisher.

This is a work of fiction. Names, characters, places, and incidents either are the product of the author's imagination or are used fictitiously, and any resemblance to actual persons, living or dead, business establishments, events, or locales is entirely coincidental.

The Author acknowledges the trademark status and trademark owners of various products referenced in this work of fiction, which have been used without permission. The publication's use of these trademarks is not authorized, associated with, or sponsored by the trademark owner.

All rights reserved.

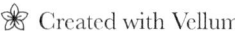 Created with Vellum

*For Nora Jean.
May you never lose your giggle,
your smile, or your light.*

AUTHOR'S NOTE

This book is not intended for, or suitable for, readers under 17. This book contains themes and scenes that are mature in nature. It also contains brief mentions of past bullying and assault. If these issues are triggering for you, please consider not reading this book.

Also, if you're related to me ... don't read this. It might make family gatherings awkward.

BROKEN

Blackwater Pack #1.5

By: Hannah McBride

1

RHODES

She was making snow angels in the dark.

It was hard not to smile. Even harder not to feel the knot around my heart twisting tighter with each beat while I watched her from the window in my bedroom. The window that looked directly into her own bedroom window next door. The windows we tried to bridge with cans and string when we were kids.

But now she was flopped on her back in the area between our yards, the moonlight bright against the fresh winter snow that had fallen earlier in the day. It gleamed off the dark ends of her hair that were visible under that ridiculously puffy white knit hat with the giant pink pompom on top.

Because of course Larkin Dawes would be making snow angels at almost midnight when the temperature had dropped into the single digits. The pure, innocent beauty of this girl never ceased to amaze me.

She looked ethereal from the light from the full moon combined with the soft glow of the Christmas lights her dad had strung all over the house and trees in their yard. She didn't need to make snow angels; she was the angel.

She carefully tried to pick herself up, moving slowly so as not to slap handprints in the angel's skirt. But, just like the last one, she still had to press a few fingers into the snow to keep her balance when standing up.

Getting to her feet, she stared at the offending marks like someone other than her own hand had put them there. Bending down, she tried to brush the smudges away, but it was pointless.

The smooth line from where she pin-wheeled her legs was broken.

With a visible sigh, Larkin straightened up, her gaze lifting towards my window and lingering.

Even though I knew there weren't any lights on, so she couldn't possibly see me, I still stepped back deeper into the shadows, which was basically the sum of our entire relationship.

Larkin played in the light. I watched from the shadows.

I was fucking tired of watching.

After another second of staring at my window, Larkin's shoulders drooped, and she headed for her back door. I waited until she was inside before turning away.

Pulling off my shirt, I balled it up and tossed it into the far corner of the room. It landed on top of the mountain of dirty clothes that had been accumulating since I came home for winter break. At some point I was going to have to do laundry or join a nudist pack.

Usually I didn't let the hamper get more than half full before washing. My room was the only place I hung out in the house, and I kept it military clean and organized. Katy had taken a psych course one year as an elective and told me

I was compensating for the chaos in my life by controlling this space I inhabited.

She was probably right. I used to clean up after dad, but that seemed to make him sadder, which led to more drinking, and more to clean up. I broke that cycle when I was in middle school, finally focusing on my room and letting the rest of the house be buried in his shit.

Dad definitely hadn't touched the laundry while I was away at school. The last load I had thrown in of his clothes, was still sitting in the washer when I came home, the moldy smell all the excuse I needed to bag them all up and throw them away for good.

The only appliance Dad ever cracked open in the house was the one that kept his beer cold. It had been stupid of me to think he might do a load of laundry.

Sighing, I opened my door and walked down the stairs quietly until I reached the living room, following the flickering light from the tv to where Dad's favorite spot was.

He was passed out in front of the tv, some serial cop procedural on adding background noise that did nothing to muffle the snores. I moved to turn off the tv, my foot kicking an empty beer can. It rolled across the dirty carpet into a pile of other cans that toppled down. It was a shitty game of bowling, but it looked like I scored a strike.

Gritting my teeth, I surveyed the layers of beer cans and bottles. This was too much to ignore; I couldn't even cross the floor without tripping over something.

I didn't even bother glaring at his unconscious form in the armchair as I started gathering the cans. I tucked as many as I could into my arms and headed for the recycling in the backyard, kicking the backdoor open with my foot.

My boots crunched against the ice and snow as I focused

on not slipping on patches that had thawed and refrozen when the sun went down. A cold gust of air kicked up as I opened the recycling can and dropped the cans into it with a loud clatter. One hit the rim and bounced out onto the snowy sidewalk.

"Rhodes?"

Shit.

"Why don't you have a shirt on?" Larkin's voice was amused and soft, a hint of a laugh punctuating her question. "It's, like, eight degrees out here."

I bent and quickly snatched up the can before spinning to face her with a grimace. I held up the can. "Late night janitorial duty."

Her face fell, her dark eyes glancing over at the back door to my house. "How's your dad doing?"

I flashed her a rueful smile even as a sharp pang slapped against the side of my ribs. I resisted the urge to crush the aluminum in my hand. "Currently passed out. But he's single-handedly keeping the liquor store open at this point. I guess that's something, right?"

She flinched, folding her arms across her chest, the sleeves of her puffy white coat making her look even smaller. "Rhodes—"

"Besides," I cut her off, not needing or wanting to hear the pity, "at least I'm getting my internship hours in."

She tilted her head to one side in confusion. "Internship?"

I winked, tossing the can into the garbage with the others. "For my future as a janitor."

With a huff, Larkin rolled her eyes. "Don't be an idiot. You're not going to be a janitor- not that there is *anything* wrong with being a janitor. It's a thankless, underpaid job that deserves more recognition."

I couldn't help the chuckle that escaped. Typical Larkin, looking out for everyone else. Kindness was embedded in her DNA.

"I'll be sure to mention that at the union meetings," I told her, shoving my hands into the pockets of my jeans.

Her gaze widened, her eyes tracking across my naked chest and exposed torso. It was a dick move, but I couldn't help flexing a pec when her gaze lingered. The blush on her cheeks was almost worth it.

The masochist in me let my brain wander to what would happen if I reached out and grabbed her, smashing her soft curves against me. I wondered if she still used the root beer flavored chapstick from when we were kids.

If I kissed her, would I taste it on my tongue? Or would I just taste Larkin?

Pure, unfiltered Larkin.

Want and need throttled to life, humming in my veins. The wolf in my chest paced, restless as always whenever Larkin was near and I let my thoughts wander. *Especially* when I let my thoughts wander.

Only problem was, that could never happen.

My wolf and I both needed to accept that.

Clearing my throat, I moved to fold my arms across my chest. God, it was really freaking cold.

"You could go to college with the rest of us," Larkin said suddenly, hope in her voice.

That hope was always my undoing. Something in her gaze shifted, a softness that melted her big brown eyes when she was about to tell me she believed in me, and that I could do anything.

Those talks gutted me. I wished like hell I could be that guy for her. If I was being honest, sometimes I wanted that for myself, too, but it wasn't in the cards. The husk of a man dead to the world inside the house was proof.

"Not really a college guy, Lark," I reminded her gruffly.

Her mouth flattened. She sucked in a deep breath, and I could see the wheels turning in that pretty head of hers. I knew Larkin well enough to know she was about to launch a verbal assault to tell me all the ways I could have a future that didn't involve a mop or an arsenal of cleaning supplies.

One of the only good things to come out of the shitshow of last semester was Larkin starting to stand up for herself. The quiet omega was finally showing that steel backbone I knew was buried deep.

I ground my molars together thinking about the root of that change.

In my nightmares, I still saw her face minutes after she had been attacked - assaulted - at school. The way her body shook, the fear in her eyes. It was enough to make me want to break something, or *someone's*, face.

Sadly, Trace had escaped and justice slipped through our fingers yet again. Larkin should have had closure, and I should have had Trace's head as a new soccer ball.

My chest burned with hate; my rage mingling with my wolf's in a volatile cocktail that left my hands trembling.

I forced myself to be still, shoving down the feelings that always started to churn when I remembered. Emotions were dangerous, especially around this girl.

Her petite nose scrunched. "But you could—"

"Unless you count all the sorority sisters who love drunken one-night stands. *That* I could be into." I smirked, cutting her off before she could start laying out all the ways I could apply myself.

She flinched, and I felt that in my soul. Yeah, I was officially an asshole.

But the sooner Larkin moved past this crush she had on me, the sooner things would go back to normal and she could move on. Maybe find someone a little - okay, a *lot* - less fucked up.

"You always do that," she murmured, shaking her head sadly. "You always play it off like a joke. You're smart, Rhodes. I could even help you study—"

"I have other things to do besides study," I interrupted firmly. Unease crawled under my skin.

Her eyes narrowed, challenging and annoyed. "Like screw every female at GPA before you graduate?"

Okay, that stung. More than it probably should have.

I'd heard it all before. Gotten the congratulatory high-fives and smiles from guys when the rumor mill circulated my newest hookup. But seeing the open disgust in Larkin's face was like trying to stop a train with my chest. It hurt like a bitch.

Larkin had moved in next door when her family relocated to our pack. I still remember sitting on the front steps of my house, watching the car pull up and out tumbled a tiny, brown-haired girl with a yellow dress and squishy pink teddy bear tucked under her arm.

She looked at the house, and then looked at mine. I could see her eyes light up, and then she was flying across the grass that separated our houses, nearly tripping in her excitement.

Larkin had barely had time to say hi before her Mom was calling her back to help them unpack. And Larkin, being

Larkin, promptly handed me her pink teddy bear for safe keeping while she went to help her parents.

I sat on the steps, terrified my dirty fingernails would mess up the soft fur of the teddy bear, until she came back ten minutes later and said we could play at my house.

My *house* wasn't an option, but there was a pretty cool tree Remy and I liked to climb out back. When I realized she probably couldn't climb in a dress, I told her we could do something else. Katy, Ainsley, and Sierra *definitely* didn't climb trees in dresses.

Larkin tucked the bear under her arm and scaled several feet before I could blink. She stared down at me, her gaze expectant, waiting for me to catch up.

Kind of like the look she was giving me now.

"That's what you think of me?" I asked softly, hating the note of vulnerability I heard in my tone. Why was it so hard with this girl? Why was Larkin always the one who could cut through the bullshit?

Probably because she was the only one who I gave a damn about. Her opinion carried more weight than even Remy's did in my world. No matter what I did, it always came back to the girl next door.

Her expression fell, her shoulders slumped. "No, Rhodes. I *don't* think that," she replied, frustrated.

I managed to get myself under control and forced a smirk, hoping like hell she didn't see how fake it was. "Good. Because I can't screw the freshmen. They're practically kids, you know?"

Instead of my words making her blush or walk away, which was what I had been aiming for, she simply grew quiet, her big brown eyes sad. Blinking fast, she turned her head, and I saw a tear fall.

Fuck me. I was definitely an asshole.

"Lark—"

She held up a hand and took a step back. "Everything's always a joke to you, isn't it? When are you going to wake up and see no one is laughing, and no one is buying it?"

I wasn't sure how to reply to that, but that ache in my chest was turning into a full-fledged stabbing pain that wouldn't be ignored.

That same pain I felt a few nights earlier when I saw Larkin kissing Kyle and then Konnor under the fucking mistletoe in the middle of town right before Christmas.

I let out a slow breath, needing like hell to fix this twisted up mess that had become our relationship. I hated this awkward tension smothering our friendship that seemed to always be there now. Maybe she couldn't be mine in the way I really wanted, but I missed her. I missed us.

Larkin had been one of my best friends for years. The distance between us sucked.

"Larkin," I started weakly, not sure where to start.

Lips pressed into a thin line, she stepped back. "Good night, Rhodes."

Pivoting on her heel, her boots crunched against the snow as she headed back inside. She closed her door gently behind her. I watched until the light went off downstairs and the light in her room turned on.

When we were little, we always kept our windows open so we could talk to each other. In the rain and winter, we used flashlights to get each other's attention. Larkin had even taken it upon herself to learn Morse code one summer and then teach it to me so we could talk, the flashing lights a beacon when my dad would drink and I felt alone as a kid.

Tonight, she pulled the curtains closed, blocking me out.

"Fuck," I swore as I kicked the trash can, hating myself in that moment even more than I usually did.

THE HAND on my shoulder made me wake up; my body jackknifed into a sitting position. I lashed out on instinct, my fist curled and ready to do damage. Another hand, stronger than mine, caught my wrist.

"Whoa, chill out, sleeping beauty," Remy said with an amused snort. He let me go when I gave him a short nod. Stepping back, he folded his arms over his chest and looked down at me.

"Asshole," I muttered, shaking my head. My hair flopped in front of my eyes and I shoved it back, glaring up at my best friend.

Remy and I had known each other almost our entire lives. We'd been best friends since before we even knew what those words meant. Which also meant I knew him almost better than I knew myself.

And right now, something was definitely happening.

"What's up?" I demanded, raking a hand through my hair and blinking away the last traces of sleep. I was glad the covers had pooled on my lap since the dream I had been having about Larkin had been suddenly interrupted. My body hadn't quite gotten the memo that it was just a dream.

"I need you to come downstairs," Remy said, his tone low and calm. His alpha voice.

My eyes narrowed. "What's going on?"

"We'll explain everything," he replied in that infuriating unhurried way he was speaking.

"We?" That caught my attention. "Is Skye with you? She okay?"

Skye Markham, Remy's mate, was another one of my closest friends, which was kind of weird considering I'd only known her for a few months. She was Larkin and Katy's best friend and Remy's ... everything. We had been friends before I dropped the ball and let her get kidnapped right in front of me.

I might have gotten a little obsessed with making sure she was okay once she woke up from her three week coma-nap. A coma she wouldn't have been in had I done my damn job as Remy's beta and protected her.

A soft smile, sickeningly in love, lifted his expression. "Skye's good. She's not here."

That was a relief.

Remy sighed, rubbing a hand across the back of his neck. "Get dressed and come downstairs."

"Rem—"

"Trust me," he said. Something in his tone made me pause.

Finally I gave him a reluctant nod, waiting for him to leave the room before I shoved the sheets off my body and headed for the small attached bathroom.

I closed the door and slapped the light switch on, glaring at the reflection in the mirror. My hair was, unsurprisingly, a mess. I was exhausted. It had taken hours for me to fall asleep, my mind insisting on replaying the scene outside with Larkin on a loop, dissecting and analyzing everything she said. Every smile, every twitch of a facial muscle. I thought of all the things I could have said, wanted to have said, but didn't.

At one point, I almost caved and went downstairs to grab

one of the beers I knew was in the fridge. I needed something to take the edge off. But the idea of sneaking past the man out cold surrounded by empty cans made my stomach sour.

No way would I use alcohol as a way out.

I wasn't my father.

By the time I finished in the bathroom, the last memories of my Larkin fantasy had faded, and I was somewhat ready to face whatever was happening downstairs.

At least that was what I thought until my feet hit the bottom of the stairs, and I saw my best friend and his dad flanking my father in the middle of our living room.

My fully dressed and showered father.

I blinked, trying to figure out if this was some twisted part of the dream I was still in. I hadn't seen my dad look this put together in over two years. Hell, I don't think I had seen him upright this year at all.

His plaid shirt was wrinkled and too big in places, and I knew the only reason his jeans stayed up was because of the belt cinched tight. But his eyes were open and alert, if a little bloodshot. His dark hair, longer than mine and streaked with silver, was still wet and had been neatly combed, tucked behind his ears.

And there was a duffel bag at his feet.

Wary, I leaned against the wall, crossing my ankles and waiting for an explanation.

"Hi, son." Dad's voice had a gravelly rasp from years of alcohol being poured down it.

"What's going on?" I asked. I stared at him, raising my brows as I waited for an answer.

Dad's fingers twitched nervously at his sides as he let out a long sigh. His head drooped as his eyes went to the floor, unable to meet my gaze.

Fucking submitting to his own son.

There was a time my dad had been one of Gabe's betas, if not his most trusted beta, in Blackwater. Then my mom left and Dad fell apart, leaving the shell of the man standing in front of me now.

Gabe clapped a firm hand on my father's bony shoulder, the gesture supportive even as Dad flinched. "Your dad is going away for a bit, Rhodes."

"Away?" I repeated.

Dad lifted his head, and my eyes narrowed at the emotion swirling in his eyes. "I'm going to get help, son. I'm going to get better."

I blinked slowly, processing the words. "Better? You're going to rehab?"

He nodded. "Gabe helped set it up."

Gabe cleared his throat. "There's a center for shifters in northern California. He'll go there for treatment for a few weeks. Maybe a few months." Gabe smiled encouragingly at my dad. "However long it takes for your dad to get back on his feet."

I had heard of the place they were talking about. There were a few different rehab facilities around the US run by shifters for shifters. Along with a lot of fun bonus features of being a shifter—increased healing, faster reflexes—also came a barrage of super strong emotions and issues that led to a lot of shifters self-medicating with alcohol and drugs.

Something stupid that felt a lot like hope swelled in me.

I squashed it down immediately.

"Good for you," I said, keeping my tone even and aloof. Rehab was a new step, but my dad had attempted to get clean several times over the years.

Considering the empty cans covering every surface and

the half-stocked fridge, I wasn't willing to go all in on his newfound sobriety.

The worst part was I could see Remy staring at me, trying to figure out where my head was. I loved my best friend, but I didn't need him here for this. He was my brother in every way but blood, but there were some things he didn't get about my life, and this was at the top of the list.

Remy had two amazing parents. He had a big family and never had to teach himself how to cobble together a dinner from stale crackers and flat ginger ale when his dad forgot to go to the store or pay the water bill.

I knew he wanted me to be happy, or at least optimistic about this, but I had done the hopeful son routine the first three times Dad tried sobriety on. It was one bitter disappointment after the next. Now I focused on moving forward, each day getting me closer to graduation when I could be done with this whole mess and move on.

Right now, I needed my dad to get out. The sooner he left, the sooner he relapsed, and the sooner my life went back to the tenuous sort of normal I could tolerate.

"Mallory and I would love for you to come and stay with us while he's gone," Gabe offered, but even he knew it was a pointless gesture.

"I'm fine here," I replied, folding my arms over my chest.

Dad stepped forward, his head still bowed. "I'm going to get better. I promise, Rhodes."

I might have believed it if I hadn't heard that at least twenty times in my life. If he hadn't still flinched when he said my fucking name.

Rhodes.

As in Margaret Elizabeth *Rhodes.*

My mom's maiden name.

Dad had insisted I be named in some way to honor my deadbeat mother before she decided a mate and a kid were too much trouble. The proudest day of his life had been when she took his name. He felt it only right that their son should bear both of their names. Which sounded great until Mommy dearest packed a bag and walked out fourteen years ago.

Growing up, Dad had rarely called me by my name. It was always 'son' or the occasional 'champ' when he was really loaded and binge watching sports. Hardly ever Rhodes, and definitely not when he was sober.

"Good for you, Dad," I said after a beat, nodding my head. "I hope this works out for you."

His face twisted slightly. "For us, son. I'm doing this for *us*."

"Good," I repeated, not sure what else there was to say. I didn't have it in me to give him a hug and wish him well. Tell him to, what? Write? Call? Ask me to come visit for family day?

Not fucking likely.

"Let's go, Tom," Gabe said softly, heading for the door.

With a nod, my dad followed him. Remy stayed behind, his dark eyes assessing everything like always.

Dad stopped in the doorway, hesitating a second before he looked back at me. "I'm sorry, Rhodes. For all of it."

I nodded once and swallowed hard, shoving down the emotions that tried to bubble to the surface. I hated that deep down, part of me was still that little boy who wanted his dad. The boy who wanted a normal family.

Most of the time I could ignore Dad or accept his bullshit for what it was. But the apologies always did me in. They were few and far between, only borne of moments of sober clarity when he would look around and realize what he had done. What he had become.

That usually led to even more drinking.

Without another word, he ducked out of the house, pulling the front door closed as he went. As soon as it shut, I exhaled loudly.

"You okay?" Remy asked, his dark eyes searching for any chink in my armor.

I pushed off the wall and headed for the kitchen. If Dad was going to be gone for a while, I was going to clean this place up.

"All good," I replied as I walked away. I went to the sink and opened the door under it, pulling out a bucket and what meager cleaning supplies we had.

"Do you know if bleach has an expiration date?" I called over my shoulder, studying the white jug for any type of number.

Remy came in behind me, but stayed in the doorway. "Why don't you come back to my place for today? We can hang out, play video games."

I knelt in front of the open cupboard, pulling out a bottle of green window cleaner I was pretty sure was supposed to be blue. "No, thanks."

"Rhodes," Remy started.

"Don't you have a mate you can hang out with?" I cut him off. Maybe bringing up Skye would get him to lay off of me. Sometimes I missed that Remy wasn't always around the way he had been before Skye came into the picture, but I couldn't hate how happy she made him.

Maybe I could distract him by dangling her like a freaking carrot. That usually worked.

Remy smirked. "She's with Larkin."

Of course.

He plowed ahead, knowing that I couldn't use her as a distraction. "Seriously, let's just—"

"Can we not, man?" I cut him off, my spine stiffening as my control started to snap. "I don't know how long this round of sober Daddy is going to last, so I'd at least like to clean this place before he comes back and adds another layer of aluminum and dirt to it."

He fell silent behind me. I knew the alpha in him wanted to help. Hell, I knew the best friend in him wanted to help.

But right now I felt too volatile. Cleaning with the most abrasive ingredients I could find until I was dizzy off the chemical haze would have to be my distraction. If I were back at GPA, I could probably find a willing female to distract me for a few hours, but right now that wasn't an option.

Not that it would have mattered.

Every girl I hooked up with, there was only one face I saw.

One face I was trying to escape.

"Why don't I help you, and then you can come back to our house for dinner?" Remy counter-offered.

I growled low in my throat, spinning on the balls of my feet to glare up at him. "Dammit, Rem—"

"Or you can be the one to tell my mom you're not coming over," he finished innocently.

That shut me up.

Mallory Holt had all but formally adopted me years ago. She was the closest thing to a mother I had. Odds were if I didn't make an appearance for her to see me in person today, she would march down here to see for herself.

I made a face at him. "Threatening me with your mom now?"

"Whatever it takes," he replied, arching a brow. "Besides, Skye's coming over for dinner, too. If she doesn't see you, you know she'll be coming over with Mom."

Fair enough. Post-abduction and coma, Skye and I had fallen into a somewhat sibling relationship. I knew her well enough to know she would be riding shotgun as Mama-Mallory drove.

I blew out a long breath. "Fine. But we need to go to the store first for supplies. I'm worried if I mix a couple of these old bottles I'll blow the damn house up."

Remy grinned knowingly, pulling his keys from his pocket. "I'll drive."

2
LARKIN

WATCHING MY BEST FRIEND SHOPPING WAS HANDS DOWN ONE of my favorite activities. I almost wished I had brought my camera to capture the wonder on her face as she looked at everything from the fluorescent lights in the ceiling to the marble tiles on the floor inside the mall.

"It's so soft," Skye said almost reverently, touching the silk sleeve of a shirt. She rubbed it between her thumb and index finger.

I couldn't stop the smile that pulled on my lips. "You should get it. That red with your dark hair would be gorgeous."

Skye immediately dropped it like it was poison and stepped back from the rack of clothes. "I have plenty of shirts."

I rolled my eyes at her playfully. "You got a gift card for Christmas," I reminded her, my eyes dropping to the small crossbody purse she wore. "The point is for you to buy yourself something with it."

Skye stepped even further away with a sigh, starting for

the exit into the center of the mall.

I caught up, linking my arm with hers. "What gives, Skywalker?" I couldn't help myself—I kind of loved the nickname Rhodes had given her.

She sighed again. How one person could put so much sadness into a single breath, I would never know.

But then I also had no idea how Skye had survived the hell of her childhood and was still a walking, talking, functioning person.

"Maybe I'll get Mom something with it," she said, hesitating and looking back at the store we had just left.

I wrinkled my nose. "Didn't your mom give *you* the gift card?"

"Yeah, but she works so hard for her money, and there isn't anything I need," Skye argued, her emerald green eyes serious as she looked at me.

I led her over to a bench and sat us both down, drawing my knee up on the bench and twisting to face her. "Skye, I don't think you're quite getting the *gift* concept. Your mom got you this so you could buy *yourself* something."

Looking down she started playing with the necklace Remy had given her a few days before Christmas at the town tree lighting. She never seemed to take it off. Every day I had seen her before and after the holiday, she had it on.

She smoothed her thumb over the crescent moon and star pendant I knew was the symbol for the Holt family, and our pack.

"It just seems like such a waste to buy something because I want it," she finally admitted, biting her lower lip. She ducked her head, the shiny curtain of brown, almost black, hair covering the side of her face.

"Skye," I said slowly, making sure I had her attention,

"your mom worked hard so she could do something special for *you*. If you try to give the gift back or buy her something with it, then it's like you're saying she made a mistake giving it to you. You guys went without so much stuff for so long, she *wants* you to be able to do this."

"This?" she repeated, frowning.

"Go shopping with your friend and buy something just because you like it," I explained gently. "Normal teenage stuff you missed out on the last few years."

"I guess," she murmured.

"You know I'm right. If Katy were here, you know she'd slap some sense into you."

That made her smile.

Katy had gone to Alaska to visit her girlfriend, Maren, for the next week. We still had two weeks left until the spring semester at Granite Peak Academy started, and neither girl was willing to go three weeks with only FaceTime and Skype as options. Katy was currently hanging out with Maren and the Brooks Ridge pack, but I knew she was only a phone call away and would set Skye straight.

Katy had that effect on people.

I held up my cell phone. "Should I call Katy and see what she says?"

With a throaty laugh, Skye pushed my phone back down. "No. There was a cute pair of boots I liked in there."

I stood up with an affirmative nod. "Yes. Boots. Let's try them on."

Skye frowned as we got up.

"What?" I asked her as we headed back into the store.

"Doesn't it seem weird to know that other people's feet might have been in your shoes?" she asked curiously. "I wonder who walked in those boots before me."

Yeah, shopping with Skye was definitely an experience.

A half an hour later, Skye was walking out of the store in her new boots. She didn't want to wait to wear them even if it meant she might have blisters from walking around the mall.

"So, are we going to talk about the giant ass elephant in the room you seem hell-bent on ignoring?" Skye asked when we stopped at the food court to eat. She sipped her coke, her eyes wide as she looked at me.

"I'm not *hell-bent*," I muttered, taking a bite of my hotdog.

"You went on a date with Kyle *and* Konnor last night," she reminded me, leaning back in her chair. "I want details."

"It was fun. I had a nice time," I told her, my voice just this side of prim.

"Nice?" she echoed, her nose wrinkling. "That sounds … hot, Lark."

I threw up my hands. "What do you want me to say? We went to dinner, went to a movie, and then I went home."

"There was no repeat kissing sans mistletoe?" she asked, quirking a brow and reminding me of the tree lighting where the twins managed to maneuver me under a sprig of mistletoe and kissed me.

I was too shocked to say no. Plus, I wanted to be kissed.

The disappointment that followed on the heels of both kisses, was more shocking than the actual kisses themselves.

Probably because as nice and cute as Kyle and Konnor were, they weren't him. And those weren't the lips I wanted on mine.

"There was no kissing," I confirmed, not wanting to admit that was because I all but jumped out of the car when they pulled up the curb by my house. I was worried a repeat kiss would be even more disappointing than the ones at the tree lighting.

I did have a nice time. Kyle and Konnor were great guys. They were kind, considerate, and definitely interested in me.

But neither guy was the one I wanted.

I ran into my house, praying Rhodes didn't see me getting out of their car. After changing, I decided to practice my snow angel technique in the yard, hoping the crisp air would give me the clarity to stop wanting what I clearly couldn't have.

So, of course, what I couldn't have chose that moment to make a shirtless appearance to yet again show me all the things I couldn't have.

"Talk to me, Larkin," Skye ordered, her expression serious.

With a groan, I leaned forward. "I really thought this would help."

"What would help?"

"Going out with Kyle and Konnor," I answered, taking a drink of my iced tea. "I wanted to prove to myself that I could move on."

"From Rhodes?" she asked quietly, her eyes soft and understanding.

I nodded. "Rhodes and I aren't a thing. We never have been. So, why the heck did it feel like I was cheating on him the entire time I was out with them?"

"Because you love him?"

"I don't *want* to love him," I said stubbornly, frowning.

Skye smiled. "Trust me. *That* I can understand."

"Says the girl with the perfect mate," I grumbled, shooting her a glare with no heat behind it. I really couldn't fault her for loving Remy.

"He is kind of perfect, isn't he?" she agreed, her eyes sparkling as she giggled. Her hand went to the throat, touching the silver pendant again. "It's kind of annoying sometimes."

"I rolled my eyes. "Yeah. You seem completely miserable."

"Why don't you just tell him how you feel?" she asked seriously after a long pause.

I froze, my heart thumping painfully in my chest. "Because."

"Because why?" she pressed, not willing to let it go.

I huffed, folding my arms over my chest. "Because he's ... *Rhodes*."

Her head jerked back and she made a face. "What does *that* mean?"

"Rhodes has been one of my best friends for as long as I can remember," I told her honestly, ignoring the way saying his name made my heart ache. "He's made it pretty clear what he expects out of relationships from the girls he's with. You know what? You can't even call them relationships. Rhodes doesn't *do* relationships. And I am the ultimate relationship girl."

Skye looked at me quizzically. "Have you ever been in a relationship?"

"Semantics," I said, waving a dismissive hand. "It's a figure of speech. Rhodes sees me like a little sister. Like a fuzzy kitten or something. Not a girl he would ..." I trailed off, blushing.

She leaned forward, resting her elbow on the table and propping her chin in the palm of her hand. "Not a girl he would *what*, Lark?"

"Screw into the floor?" I said with a helpless shrug, my cheeks heating.

She barely blinked. "Do you *want* him to screw you into the floor?"

Yes. Please, God, yes.

"I don't know," I mumbled, embarrassed and flustered. I couldn't help but think back to last night when I talked to Rhodes outside.

And he didn't have a shirt on.

Coming up behind him, I had a good chance to study his back and the hard muscles roped across his shoulders. I thought my tongue would fall out of my mouth when he turned around and I saw his chest.

Rhodes was all male perfection. Just the right amount of muscle and all of it defined, from the ridges of his abdomen to the hard planes of his chest. What really did me in was the sharp lines above his hip bones that formed a perfect 'v' all pointing down, down, down.

"Hmm," she hummed. "Your mouth says no, but your red checks and heavy breathing say hell yes."

I swirled the straw in my cup. "You know, sometimes, I imagine telling him I've been in love with him since I was little, and I want to be with him."

Skye pressed her lips together but didn't say anything.

I let out a shaky laugh. "And then I think of him laughing at me. Or worse, looking at me with pity. Either way, it would ruin our friendship."

"Rhodes would never laugh at you," Skye said gently. She reached across the table and took my hand in hers.

She was right. One of the things I loved most about him was how much he joked and looked for the fun in everything, but he also knew when to be serious. When I was eleven and my grandma died, he snuck into my room every night for a week to make sure I fell asleep okay.

I think that was when I fell in love with him.

Rhodes wouldn't laugh because deep down he was a

good guy.

"The idea that I might lose Rhodes in my life is too much," I whispered. "I'll deal with my feelings as long as it means I get to keep him as my friend."

Her hand squeezed mine. "I still think you should talk to him. You might be surprised."

I gave her a smile in return, knowing there was no way I would ever lay my emotions at Rhodes' feet. Whatever pieces of my heart still functioned would be decimated if Rhodes turned me down.

"How have you been sleeping?" I asked suddenly, needing to change the subject before I started crying.

Skye blinked. It was like watching the gate in a castle lower behind her eyes as she locked down her feelings.

"Fine."

"I can still call Katy," I reminded her, only half-kidding.

Her lips twisted in a bitter, humorless smile. "Okay. Some nights are better than others."

"Is Remy still coming over at night?"

Sighing, she nodded. "My mom would probably freak if she knew he spent the night with me almost every night."

I reached across the table for her hand. "Skye, you almost died. You were kidnapped by a guy who spent his life terrorizing you. I think you're allowed to want your mate with you."

"I hate night time," she whispered, fury heating her words. "It's like when the sun goes down—"

"—the monsters get the scariest," I finished for her. I knew that. I lived that.

"Yeah." Her mouth turned down. "Remy doesn't even wait for me to call him now. He just shows up. I don't even lock my window anymore so he can get in whenever."

"Having a tree outside your window is convenient for late-night visitors," I added with a shrug.

She traced the ring of condensation around her drink with a finger. "I do think it's getting better. I mean, I'm having less nightmares."

"That's good."

"But when I do have them…" She trailed off, her eyes clouding over before she shivered. "It's not even the same nightmares. Sometimes I'm in Long Mesa, sometimes I'm on the cliff … Sometimes I'm in bed with Remy, and then suddenly it's Cassian there instead."

I nodded, swallowing roughly. I totally understood that. I still had nightmares from when Trace had cornered me in a bathroom during a dance. The feral look in his eyes, the tearing sounds of the fabric when he ripped my dress, hands groping…

Night was always the worst. It was when memories twisted into a reality I couldn't escape.

"But it's better when Remy's there?"

She nodded. "Yeah. I mean, I know Cassian's dead. Everyone who was there said he didn't survive the fall. But maybe if I had seen his … body," she grimaced, "or something, I would know it's real?"

"Maybe go to his grave?" I offered. That sounded even stupider when I spoke it out loud than when I thought it.

She huffed out a laugh. "If I knew where it was, I might."

When Cassian and Skye went over the cliff, the main focus had been Skye and saving her. While Trace and his allies escaped, they had taken Cassian's body with them to cover up that he had ever been there and that the Norwood pack was involved.

"Besides, he's probably buried in Long Mesa. It's not exactly on my road-trip list." Skye sipped her drink.

"I wish you could have closure," I murmured sadly.

Her serious gaze met mine and held.

My wolf squirmed inside of me, and after a beat, I looked away.

It was amazing anyone could have ever mistaken Skye for an omega.

"You never got your closure either," she reminded me softly. "How are *you* doing?"

"I'm—" I stopped when I saw her raise an eyebrow. "I'm better. I still have nightmares, too, but they're not like they were. Besides, Trace is gone. At least I won't have to deal with him next semester, or ever again."

She touched my wrist. "I'm here if you ever want to talk. You know that, right?"

Sniffling, I pulled back and tried to wipe my eyes without her noticing while nodding. The movement had me looking out the windows of the food court where I could see the skies growing grayer.

"Looks like that storm is coming sooner rather than later," I remarked, jumping at the chance to change the subject.

Skye's eyes followed mine, letting me out of the conversation. "Oh, wow. Should we go?"

"Sure," I said, gathering my bags. "Am I still taking you to Remy's?"

She nodded, picking up her one shopping bag. I tried not to sigh at the difference.

"Mallory asked me to come for dinner. Remy will drive me home later," she replied. "You're welcome to stay, too."

I shook my head. "Thanks, but I'm good. Since my

parents are gone, I'm going to curl up in front of the tv with a movie and ice cream."

"Sounds fun." Skye smiled at me as we started walking back towards where I parked the car. "Your parents went to … Iowa?"

"Idaho," I corrected with a laugh. "They're visiting my Aunt Lucy, who is my mom's best friend."

"You didn't want to go?"

I shook my head. "No. I'm enjoying the peace and quiet. Plus, I still need to finish my independent study report so I can get the extra English credits I need to graduate this spring."

She hip checked me with a warm chuckle. "Dork."

"Maybe." I shrugged and dug the car keys out of my pocket as we headed for the doors. "Have you started working on your college applications?"

Skye groaned, pushing the door open as we stepped out into the cold. "Yes. Remy's helping, but it's taking forever. They want an essay on my hardest challenge I've faced. I'm not sure writing about growing up in a whorehouse and killing two people is what they have in mind, though."

I unlocked the car and tossed my bags in the back seat of the Jeep my parents let me use when I was home. "You definitely have more life experiences than most. Don't forget your three week coma. I bet other people can't use that in their application."

Laughing, she got into the car and shut the door. I got in on my side and started the car, blasting the heater.

"It still feels surreal, you know? The idea that I might be going to college?" She rubbed her hands together and wouldn't look at me.

"It's not an idea," I corrected, putting the Jeep in gearing and pulling out of the spot. The West Falls Mall was about twenty miles outside of Blackwater, but the roads were mostly empty as people stayed home, preparing for the impending snow storm.

"You're *going* to college," I told her firmly. "You, me, Katy, Remy – we're all going."

"And Rhodes?" she added.

I snorted. "Rhodes is one of the smartest guys I know, but he seems determined to wallow in unfulfilled potential."

Skye burst out into a fit of laughter. "'Wallow in unfulfilled potential?' Maybe it's time to lay off the thesaurus."

I slapped her shoulder as I merged onto the road. "Hush, you."

The drive back to Blackwater was fast with no traffic and Skye keeping me laughing the whole way back. As much fun as shopping with her was, watching her listen to songs on the radio was even better.

Snow was starting to fall as I pulled up in front of the Alpha house at the top of the mountain. I put the car in park, ignoring the kick to my heart when I saw Rhodes catch a football that one of Remy's brothers launched at him. All four looked to be in the middle of a game of football, that Remy quickly abandoned when he saw us pull in.

The Jeep had barely stopped before Skye was getting out and sliding into Remy's arms as he pulled her from the inside of the Jeep with a grin.

"Have fun?" he asked her softly, his hands coming up to frame her face.

"Yeah," she answered with a smile, lifting to her tiptoes to kiss him.

Smiling, I looked away. My expression froze when I saw

Rhodes staring at me, his hand curled around the football at his side.

"Hey, Larkin."

Remy's greeting made me jump. I turned and looked at him. "Hey, yourself. I better get going. The storm's coming in faster than I thought."

A light coat of snow already covered the road behind me.

Skye wrapped an arm around Remy's waist, pressing herself to his side. "Are you sure you don't want to stay?"

I shook my head. "I should get home before it really starts coming down." I hated driving in snow, even in a four wheel drive vehicle.

"Can you give me a ride?" Rhodes asked, coming up to the open passenger door.

"I thought you were staying for dinner," Remy said with a frown.

Rhodes shook his head. "I'll catch a ride home with Larkin. That way you don't have to drive me back."

"I'm already driving Skye home," Remy reminded him. "It's no big deal to drop you off, too."

Rhodes jumped into the vacant passenger seat, pulling on the seatbelt. "Skye lives in town, and I'm the opposite direction. I'll catch up with you later."

"You sure?"

Rhodes nodded. He grinned at Skye. "How's it going, Skywalker?"

"Pretty good, Rhodey," she replied with a warm smile. She reached out, briefly touching his arm as he walked by. "Call us if you need anything?"

"Will do," he replied quickly, closing the door. He gave me a smile. "Ready?"

I put the vehicle in gear and spun us around to drive back

down the mountain. Halfway down, snow was falling even heavier and the road was completely covered.

"I can drive if you don't want to," Rhodes offered, his tone nonchalant as he glanced at me.

My hands tightened around the wheel. "I think I'm okay."

"You're choking the steering wheel, baby girl."

"So I can control the car, Rhodes," I snapped, ignoring the nickname he had used for years, but rarely called me anymore. I was too stressed to think about that. I filed it away to mentally unpack tonight when I was safe in my bed.

My knuckles ached from the deathgrip I had on the leather. I really hated driving in snow.

"You're doing fine," he said gently. "But I don't mind driving."

I made it to the bottom of the mountain and put the car in park at the stop sign. I refused to look at Rhodes as I undid my seatbelt. "Okay, you drive."

To his credit, Rhodes didn't crack any jokes. He got out of the Jeep, coming around the front and opening my door.

"Sorry," I muttered, sliding down until my feet touched the ground. It was so stupid. How could I not drive three freaking miles?

"Hey," he said softly, his index finger tipping my chin up to look at me.

I blinked as a snowflake caught on my lashes.

"You did great," he told me, his voice soft and warm. "It's fine, Lark."

"I'm a wimp," I replied, my shoulders drooping.

His lips curved into an adorable smile. "No, you're not. You just don't like driving in shitty weather."

"Thanks," I murmured, tilting my head back a little more

to look at him.

His dark eyes were unreadable as he looked down at me, and for just a second, I thought I saw his gaze dip to my mouth. I licked my lips as anticipation zipped through me, the pull strong enough to sway me on my feet.

His eyes definitely caught that. He swallowed roughly, and I realized how close we were standing together as snow swirled around us on the empty street.

"We should get going," he said softly, stepping back. A gust of cold wind chilled me as it whipped into the vacant space between our bodies, chilling me more effectively than any cold shower.

Clearing my throat, I stepped around him and walked around to the passenger side, climbing in. He put the Jeep in drive as I clicked my seatbelt into place.

"Are your parents home?" he asked after several minutes of silence. "I haven't seen them in a few days."

"They went to visit my aunt in Idaho," I told him.

"Right," he mused. "You didn't want to go this year?"

"I wanted to stay home," I replied, not wanting to get into the whole extra credit thing. I almost rolled my eyes. I could practically hear him call me a nerd in my head. That one word would seem so offensive to most, but he had always said it with warmth that made me feel gooey and special.

I wasn't a nerd; I was pathetic.

"How was your Christmas?" I asked, trying to switch topics.

"Good," he replied with a shrug, turning onto a side street. "Quiet. I stayed home."

"You should've come over," I replied, looking out the window. Every year my family asked Rhodes to spend the holiday with us, but every year he declined.

He was too good a guy to leave his dad alone for the holiday, even if the latter was too unconscious to know the day had any special meaning.

"How's your dad?" I questioned gently. It bugged the hell out of me that Rhodes' dad couldn't be bothered to act like a parent.

Rhodes was quiet for a long minute. "He's gone, actually."

"Gone?" I repeated dumbly, my head swinging around to study him in profile.

His jaw clenched, his hand flexing around the steering wheel. "He went to rehab."

Shock washed over me, and then total joy for him. "Rhodes, that's amazing!"

He grunted in reply.

"That's *not* amazing?" I asked slowly, trying to read his blank expression.

He shrugged. "It's whatever. We'll see if it sticks."

"Maybe it will," I said in a small voice, wanting to be hopeful for him.

He pulled onto our street. "Maybe." He pulled onto the driveway in front of my house, putting the car in park. He raked a hand through his long hair and glanced at me.

I took a deep breath. "Rhodes-"

He opened the door. "I'll see you later, Lark. Call me if you need anything."

The door slammed shut, rocking the Jeep, and I watched him walk across the front yard to his house. He stomped up the stairs, trying to knock the snow from his boots, before going inside.

With a sigh, I reached over and killed the engine, pulling keys out and heading into my own house.

3

RHODES

The sun was way too freaking bright. I groaned and rolled over, not wanting to wake up, but knowing I would have to at least get up and close the blinds if I wanted any kind of shot at going back to sleep for a few more hours.

I definitely needed sleep.

Staying up until one in the morning, replaying the car ride home with Larkin was a special sort of self-torture. I analyzed every glance, every word from her. And that wasn't counting the way her body swayed into mine when we stood on the side of the road.

I had almost kissed her.

The sad, defeated look in her eyes when I stepped back, killed me.

If this kept up I was going to be able to host my own talk show soon.

I got up, damn near tripping on the covers. Kicking them away, I crossed the few feet to the window and reached up to jerk the shade down, and I froze.

"Whoa."

The forecast had called for roughly eight to ten inches of snow, but the massive blanket of white that was easily as high as the bushes on the side of Larkin's house said the weather man had definitely misjudged. There was easily a foot and a half out there, and it was still coming down at a steady rate.

I stood at the window and watched for a second. It was peaceful, the way the snow drifted down, covering the world in a silent blanket. Everything was still and calm like one of the Christmas songs squawked about.

The sharp chime of my phone cut through that calm pretty damn quick.

Turning, I grabbed it off my desk and hit the 'talk' button when I saw it was the girl who consumed my thoughts.

"Lark?"

"Hey."

My eyes snapped up to the house next door. Larkin was standing in her bedroom window, cell phone tucked between her ear and shoulder. She was wearing a matching set of pink plaid pajamas that made me smile as she waved at me.

This girl.

"Everything okay?" I asked, bracing a hand on the wall beside the window.

She nodded, her finger drawing a heart in the condensation on the window. "I was going to make pancakes. Since it looks like we aren't going anywhere anytime soon, I thought I would see if you wanted some, too?"

My stomach growled on cue. I should say no. Turn around and go back to bed.

My stomach clenched as the thought of my *bed* while talking to *Larkin* took a decidedly graphic detour.

"Sure," I answered, wincing at my slightly strangled reply. I cleared my throat. "Let me take a shower, and I'll be over?"

"Sounds good," she said, ending the conversation and spinning away from the window.

I dropped my phone back onto the desk and groaned. It was definitely going to be a cold shower.

Hell, I should probably just go roll around in a snow drift. That might stand a chance at cooling me off.

☪

THE SNOW WAS ALREADY UP past my knees as I trudged through the yard between our houses. It took a while to move through it and once I made it to Larkin's porch, I brushed off the snow as best as I could, toeing off my boots and leaving them outside so they wouldn't track snow and ice into the foyer.

I opened the door, not surprised Larkin had left it unlocked for me.

Growing up her parents made it clear I had, what they called, open door privileges. I think they felt bad that I was pretty much on my own at home so they welcomed me into theirs. If Remy's parents were my stand in parents, Larkin's were my stand in aunt and uncle.

They just sucked at hiding their worry and pity a little more than the Holts.

Charles and Jane Dawes had a perfect family, a perfect daughter, and a happy life. She was a teacher, he was an accountant. Their house was always clean, warm, and smelled like some fancy candle had been burning.

Yet another reason why my train wreck of a family and Larkin's would never mix. Even if Dad kicked the alcohol and made it through this stint in rehab, I didn't see my dad and Larkin's parents sitting down over dinner together.

And Larkin would definitely want family dinners.

I closed the door behind me, and grabbed the towel she had left on the small table, using it to dry off the bottoms of my jeans as best as I could before heading down the hallway that opened into a large kitchen.

Larkin stood at the stovetop, a pop song blaring from the bluetooth speaker on the counter. I watched, fascinated, as she shimmied her hips and moved her tiny feet. Her dark hair had been pulled into a messy knot on top of her head, and it bounced along with the bopping of her head as she used a spatula as a microphone she could lip-sync into.

Larkin had a ton of amazing qualities – she was a loyal friend, a genius when it came to school, an amazing photographer – but the girl had absolutely no rhythm. I also knew, from painful experience, that she couldn't carry a tune to save her life.

Yet, she loved music in almost any form.

She attempted a slide across the kitchen floor, but misjudged the momentum. With a small shriek she started to fall, her feet slipping out from under her. I jumped forward, catching her under her arms and hauling her against me before her ass could hit the tiles.

"Crap," she whispered, arching her neck back to look up at me. She gave me a brilliant Larkin grin, so sweet and guileless it was a solid blow to my chest.

She smelled like cinnamon and sugar, her soft hair tickling my nose. I knew I should let her go, but it felt good to hold her soft body against mine, to feel the way her curves molded around me. Her weight in my arms felt right.

It had been a long time since I was this close to her. Larkin loved to hug, and I caught on earlier this year that my body loved the way she hugged. I had taken to avoiding her hugs out of self-preservation.

Okay, *dick* preservation.

Only one of my heads seemed to get that Larkin was off-limits.

Clearing my throat, I made sure she was steady on her feet before letting go and taking a large step back. I leaned back against the counter across from her.

Space. We definitely needed space.

Larkin was still grinning at me, completely oblivious to the war I was fighting internally.

"Pancakes are almost done," she said, swinging back around to the stove and picking up a spatula. "Can you grab—"

I was already pushed off the counter and moving to the fridge to pull out the orange juice I knew she would want.

Extra pulp.

I made a face as I pulled it out, also grabbing the no pulp one her parents kept on hand for me. Grabbing a couple of cups out of the overhead cabinet, I poured the drinks as she finished plating the last of the pancakes.

We met at the kitchen table and sat down in front of the large bay window that showcased the snowy backyard.

"I can't believe it's still coming down," she commented, looking outside before reaching for the syrup and essentially drowning her pancakes in a river of sugar. "I checked the weather this morning. Sounds like they may upgrade it to a blizzard."

My gaze flicked to the window where the larger flakes from earlier had been replaced by a finer, but blinding, snow. "There's almost two feet out there. I think they're a bit late on that call."

Larkin's eyes went wide a second before she took a big bite. "I haven't seen any snow plows out yet."

"They're probably sticking to the mountain and town," I replied, taking a drink. What limited snow plows Blackwater had typically made sure the roads around the Alpha house were clear in case Gabe was needed for anything.

"What are you going to do today?" she asked suddenly.

The question caught me off guard. "I don't know. Maybe work on my bike." I had been slowly rebuilding a 1990 Harley Fat Boy for the last year whenever I was home. I had always loved engines and mechanics, but this was definitely the biggest project I had taken on. It was currently in a few hundred pieces around the floor of the garage.

"Can I help?"

I looked up, and my fork froze in midair at her small voice.

Larkin shifted on her seat, looking down. "I mean, unless I'll be in the way."

She wouldn't be.

Larkin was a pretty damn amazing assistant. She had helped me with more oil changes and brake replacements then I could count. My house had become a secondary garage in Blackwater, and a lot of people asked me to do routine maintenance on their vehicles because I would do it for a lot cheaper than the local garage.

I had been doing it since I was thirteen. Larkin was usually there, oil and grease smeared on her cheeks, working alongside me. Most girls wouldn't be caught dead with motor oil under their nails.

Larkin wasn't most girls.

She would have spent all her time in the garage with me

if I had let her. This past summer, I had stopped inviting her to help all to maintain that damn distance between us.

I lifted the bite of food to my mouth and started chewing, swallowing before I answered. "Sure. If you want."

Her shoulders visibly relaxed, another smile blossoming on her lips.

She had expected me to say no.

The food in my stomach turned into a solid mass I couldn't get rid of. I pushed my plate away and finished my drink.

I should have said no. I should have gone back to my house and left her alone here.

"Have you heard from your dad yet?"

My back went rigid, my shoulders stiff. "No," I replied, my tone clipped. There was a message waiting on my cell that had appeared when I was in the shower, but I hadn't even considered listening to it.

She pressed her lips together in a thin line. "Is it weird? Him not being home?"

I sighed. "It's different." I looked up and grinned at her. "Definitely cleaner."

She sadly shook her head, not buying my act for a damn second. She knew me too well. "You don't have to do that, Rhodes."

Her nostrils flared delicately. Jesus, even her *nostrils* were cute. Attached to an adorable button nose that wrinkled whenever she was laughing or worried or over-thinking.

I needed to get a hold of my emotions and lock them down fast.

"Do what?" I replied blankly, grinding my molars together.

She huffed, pushing her plate away. "I know, okay? You don't have to pretend with me."

"Who's pretending?" I snapped, spreading my arms wide. Irritation flashed through me at being so transparent. "I'm *fine*, Lark. It's just another day."

"But your dad is trying to get better," she argued, her dark eyes flashing. "I know that has to mean something to you."

"It doesn't mean shit to me!" I exploded, getting up so fast the chair damn near toppled over. "I've heard the 'I'm going to get better, son' speech eleven times. *Eleven* times. You know how many times it stuck?"

She stayed quiet, watching me as all the emotions I had buried and shoved down came up and out like the force of a volcanic explosion.

"I'm done waiting for him to be a father. I've lived the last fourteen years without a parent, and he wants to pick *now* as the time to step up? I'm supposed to believe this is different than every other single time?" I paced away from the table, my fists clenched.

"I know he's not going to change," I ranted, stomping across the room and bracing my hands on the counter. I dropped my chin, squeezing my eyes shut as I tried to get control of myself. "It's stupid and pointless to think he will."

"You mean, it's stupid and pointless to get your hopes up?" Larkin countered softly.

I spun around to see she was right behind me. I hadn't even heard her get up.

I opened my mouth, ready to tell her how wrong she was, but the look in her eyes stopped me.

Not pity. Not sadness. Her dark eyes were filled with kindness and hope.

The two things that Larkin was to the very core.
Two things I fucking loved about her.
I swallowed thickly as I looked down at her. She was less than a foot away. It wouldn't take much effort to reach out and haul her small body against mine. To cross that last line that separated us.

"There's nothing to hope for," I admitted, my voice cold and hard even to my own ears. "It's stupid to want something that can *never* happen."

Something changed in her expression, a fleeting glimpse of a deeper emotion she quickly hid away from me. Damn, I wished I had the right to demand she tell me what was on her mind. I wanted to know every thought that went through her beautiful mind.

"Hope is never stupid, Rhodes," she told me softly, reaching out and touching my wrist.

Jesus, her hands were so tiny compared to mine. So delicate and soft. Mine were rough and hard from years of working in the garage.

I blinked slowly, working to put my feelings back into the bottle they belonged in. "It is when you know the outcome will never change."

She shifted forward, barely half a step, but it was enough that I caught the scent of cinnamon and sugar that clung to her. I could see the way each dark lash framed her eyes, eyes that held a ring of liquid gold around the pupils. I could make out the tiny freckles across the bridge of her nose.

"Things change all the time," she said, her voice gentle and soothing. A freaking balm on the jagged, brittle edges of my heart that was making it harder to remember I was supposed to be the good guy and let her move on.

I closed my eyes. "Lark—"

Her hand left me, and I felt the air rush between us as she moved back. "Let's get this cleaned up and you can show me what you've done to the motorcycle."

She turned and started clearing our dishes off the table before I could respond.

Not that I would have even known what to say if I could find my voice.

I was quickly realizing we were running out of words to say to keep up this distant charade.

4

LARKIN

THE GARAGE WAS BARELY WARMER THAN OUTSIDE, BUT THE little heater Rhodes had plugged in while he sat on the floor of the garage working on his bike helped. Kind of.

I was still freaking freezing.

I sat a few feet away on an overturned bucket next to the open toolbox. I wasn't sure what half of the little parts spread on the tarp in the bike did, but I wasn't too concerned about all those little pieces.

I was too busy staring at the way Rhodes was stretched out on his back, his shirt riding up to show those indents on his hips and a thin trail of dark hair disappearing into his jeans. He grunted as he tightened something that was probably important.

All I knew was it did awesome things for his arms in that shirt, the edges on the t-shirt clinging to his muscles.

I reached for the bottle of water at my feet, trying to keep from swallowing my tongue.

"Can you hand me the flat head screwdriver?" he called,

letting his head fall back against the floor as he studied the machine over him.

I plucked it from the tool box, leaned forward and placed it into his open palm.

"Thanks." Another grunt that did weird things to my stomach.

"So, what are you going to do with this one?" I asked, my hands clinging to the plastic bottle in my hands. I was glad for the cold since it was the only way my body was cooling down anytime this century.

His arm stretched higher, pulling up more of his shirt.

And there's abs one and two, making their first appearance to today's programming.

I barely caught myself from licking my lips.

I was such a masochist.

Why had I thought it would be a good idea to be trapped in this little garage with the guy I had only been in love with for the last five years?

"Not sure," he replied, distracted. His other arm reached around to grab something.

Abs three and four, ladies and gentlemen.

"I think I'm going to keep this one," he continued, completely unaware that all my girl parts were about to stage a revolt and divorce my brain.

I shivered, and not from the cold. My wolf volunteered to take over if I couldn't get my hormones under control.

I closed my eyes, focused on breathing through my mouth so I couldn't inhale any particle of his scent.

"Keep it?" I echoed, trying to focus on something that was not skin or muscle.

"Yeah. Might be fun to have a bike." He finished tightening the screw and slid out from under the motorcycle, sitting up smoothly and looking at me. "Obviously not now, but in the summer, it would be amazing."

I found myself nodding. "It would be pretty awesome."

He reached for the rag at his side, wiping his hands. "Besides," he said, his brown eyes flashing at me before he winked suggestively, "chicks dig a guy on a motorcycle."

The cold in the garage instantly settled into my bones, a block of ice forming in the pit of my stomach as I imagined Rhodes speeding down a winding mountain road with some nameless girl's arms and legs wrapped around him.

I barely suppressed a growl. I wasn't sure if it was me or my wolf that was more offended by the idea. My head dropped as I rubbed my forehead.

Focus, Larkin.

He cleared his throat. "Or maybe I'll sell it. I could use the money as a down payment to get an apartment in town."

My head came up so fast I got dizzy. "You're moving?"

He got to his feet and crossed the garage floor to the workbench on the far wall, digging through a jar that held loose screws and nails. "Yeah. After graduation, I'll be eighteen. I'll get a place in town. I already talked to Harry. He said he would hire me at the garage."

"What about college?"

His shoulders stiffened for a second before he turned and came back, dropping to a crouch on the other side of the bike. His eyes met mine over the seat. His lips were smiling, but his eyes were flat.

"I told you, Lark," he said, "I'm not a college kind of guy." He gestured to the bike. "*This* I'm good at."

"You're good at a lot of things," I blurted out.

His eyes widened for a fraction of a second before he

chuckled and went back to working. "You're a good friend, Larkin. But we both know I suck at school."

"Because you don't try," I retorted. "But that's all an act, and we both know it, Rhodes. You're one of the smartest people I know."

He gave me a strange look.

"I told you I could help you study," I finished sadly.

All he offered was a tight-lipped smile. "Thanks. But I think I'm good."

I wanted to argue. Wanted to shake his amazingly broad shoulders until he admitted I was right and decided he was going to apply to college.

Preferably the same one I was going to be at.

"What time is it?"

I glanced down at my watch. "A little after two."

"Are you hungry?" he asked, looking up.

I shrugged. "Not really. The pancakes were a lot."

He nodded.

"But you're hungry," I guessed. Rhodes was a bottomless pit. The last three years, Mom had taken to adding extra food to the pantry because Rhodes had been over so often.

She still did that, even though he hadn't been over much the last year.

He grinned wryly at me. "You know me so well."

I laughed. "Want me to go make you something?"

He dropped the wrench he had been using and stood up, stretching his arms up over his head to work out the kinks.

Look quick, folks! The rarely viewed abs five and six have just made an unexpected cameo!

With a sigh, I forced my eyes shut.

"You okay?"

I opened my eyes to see Rhodes staring at me, his face

creased with concern. But at least his arms were at his sides and his shirt was where it was supposed to be.

Shaking my head, I stood up. "I'm fine. Headache or something. Maybe the weather. A drop in barometric pressure or, you know, temperature."

I was babbling.

Stop. Refocus. And, go.

"So, food?" I gave him a too-bright smile, attempting the fastest change of subject in the history of the world.

He smiled slowly, nodding in agreement before he paused and made a face.

"Why don't I take a shower first?" He held his hands out in front of him. They were black with grease and grime.

"You're done?" I asked as I looked around the floor. Half the bike was still scattered around us. I'm glad he knew what the final picture of this puzzle looked like, because I was completely lost.

"For today," he replied. His lips hooked into a devastating grin that made my knees a little weak. "Hey, Lark, how much do you love me?"

That was a loaded question I didn't think either of us was ready to tackle.

But I already knew where his mind was headed. "You want me to make you spaghetti?"

He flashed a row of even, white teeth at me, shaking his hair out of his eyes. "If you're offering."

This boy had a serious love affair with carbs. He never missed spaghetti night at my house when Mom made it. In the last year, she had been teaching me her recipes. Spaghetti was one of the first things she taught me. It was my dad's favorite so we always had the ingredients for it on hand.

I rolled my eyes. "Fine. I'll go make food. You go shower. You stink."

Something wild and playful lit his eyes and, for a second, I thought he would lunge and grab me. It was definitely something I would have expected from Rhodes a few months ago.

But the light dimmed and then extinguished completely.

He rocked back on his feet with a tight smile, hooking his thumbs absently in his belt loops. "Cool. I'll meet you back at your place?"

I nodded, heading for the side door of the garage. I pushed against it, but it wouldn't budge. Looking out the small window, I could see the snow had piled up even more.

"Um, Rhodes?"

He was across the garage and at my side in a second. "What's wrong?"

I tried the door again. "It's stuck."

He craned his neck to look over my shoulder, peering out the window. "Whoa. That's crazy."

"I guess I'll go out the front door," I said, stepping back and right into a wall of muscle.

Okay, I had definitely lied.

He smelled amazing. Like diesel engines and something masculine that was just Rhodes. Thankfully the cold garage kept him from being a sweaty mess.

His hand fell to my hip on instinct, steadying me as I swayed on my feet. His long fingers tensed, tightening for a fraction on the waistband of my jeans.

Quickly he jerked his hand away.

"Shit, sorry. I think I just ruined your jeans."

"It's fine," I murmured, brushing by him. I was never washing these jeans again.

I might have accidentally let my butt brush against him as I moved around his body. And I might have smirked a bit when he sucked in a sharp breath.

My wolf hummed her approval as I headed to the door that led inside and opened it. I could walk through his house blindfolded and never hit a thing, that's how well I knew it. Rhodes used to come up with any excuse for me not to come over until I finally made it clear I didn't care what it looked like or how wasted his dad was.

The living room was definitely cleaner as I made my way through it to the main hall. I could hear Rhodes coming in behind me as I pulled the door open to a frigid blast of arctic air.

"Shit," I muttered, grabbing my coat from where it hung on the bannister. I quickly pulled it on and headed out into the snow.

It took an eternity to cross the space between our yards. By the time I got into the house, I had waded through snow almost mid-thigh. My jeans were coated in the white powder as I stepped inside.

Shutting the door, I quickly stripped out of my jeans and walked down the hall to the laundry room, tossing them in the large sink basin there so the snow could finish melting off. My gaze lingered on the smudges of grease on the waistband before I snapped myself out of it. I hurried up the stairs, freezing my butt off before making it into my room and grabbing a pair of leggings and tugging them on.

I was halfway through making the spaghetti sauce when Rhodes let himself in.

"It's *freezing*," he muttered, coming into the kitchen.

Apparently he had the same idea I did because he headed

back for the laundry room with what looked like a pair of extra jeans in a plastic grocery bag.

I counted the number of times my spoon made a full circle around the edge of the pot. Anything to not think about the fact that Rhodes was taking his pants off on the other side of the wall.

"Can I help?" he asked, coming back into the room.

I jerked my head to the pantry. "Grab the noodles?"

This had become a timeless dance we both knew the steps to instinctively.

I chopped veggies, he got out the plates. I stirred the sauce, he started boiling water. Each action by one of us had a counter reaction by the other that was so simply domestic it made my heart ache.

Why couldn't everything with us be this freaking easy?

We made stupid small talk as we worked, and by the time we sat down to eat, I was ready to snap if he mentioned the weather one more time.

For a minute there in the garage, it was like old times.

Now in the quiet house, it felt like we were being smothered by all the unspoken things hanging between us.

We ate in silence for several minutes before my phone chirped at the end of the table. Rhodes reached for it and passed it to me, but not before seeing the name lighting up on the screen.

KYLE MCALLISTER

His fingers tightened around the glass and plastic before he all but shoved it into my waiting hand.

His fork scraped against his plate, the sound setting my teeth on edge.

"Kyle, huh?" Rhodes finally grunted, not looking at me.

I set the phone down without opening the message. "Yeah. We're ... friends."

Another grunt. "Friends, huh?"

My hackles rose, my eyes narrowing as I glared at him. "Yes, Rhodes. We're *friends*. Friends text each other."

"And apparently kiss each other," he muttered under his breath.

"Ex*cuse* me?" I set my fork down and leaned back in my chair. "What does that mean?"

He looked up at me with a blank, almost bored, expression. "I'm just saying. I saw you two at the tree lighting. Or, should I say you *three*."

I folded my arms and waited, knowing he wasn't done.

Rhodes braced his forearms on the table. "I never pegged you for a ménage kind of girl, Lark."

My eyes went wide. "That's a healthy dose of judgement coming from the manwhore of GPA."

A muscle in his jaw jumped as he clenched his teeth. "You're not that kind of girl, Larkin. *That's* all I meant."

"And what kind of girl am I?" I snapped. Anger blazed like a furnace in me. "That's right. I'm supposed to be good, old Larkin. The girl who sits back and has zero life."

He breathed deeply through his nose. "That's not what I'm saying."

"Then what *are* you saying?" I demanded. I balled my hands into fists to keep them from shaking.

He sighed. "You're a *good* girl."

My jaw dropped open. "So, that means what? That I can't date? Kiss a guy?"

Or two.

He snorted, pushing back from the table. "By all means,

do whatever the hell you want with whoever the hell you want."

I sucked in a sharp breath. "Is it so hard to believe someone, or *two* someones, are interested in me?"

"I didn't say that," he snapped, raking a hand through his hair. His eyes flashed. A hint of darkness that shouldn't have thrilled me the way it did.

It made me crave more.

"Or am I supposed to join a convent and wear a chastity belt to make you happy?" I retorted, months of pent up frustration and anger fueling me as I broke. "Is good little Larkin supposed to stay a virgin forever to keep you happy?"

Okay, that might have been too far, but I was hoping he would think the redness on my cheeks was from anger and not bashfulness.

Rhodes tossed his napkin onto the table and stood up suddenly, retreating from the conversation and me. "Wow. You know what? Forget I said anything."

I stood up just as fast, recklessly needing to get this out. "I guess I should be glad you're finally saying *something* to me."

He whirled, dark eyes narrowing. "What the hell does that mean?"

"It means I've noticed how you've made a point to push me away since last summer," I snapped, finally letting it all out. I came around the table and stopped in front of him, giving him a small shove. "You've spent the last few months running away from me so many times it gave me whiplash!"

His dark eyes glittered, his chest heaved. "Larkin—"

"No!" I cut him off. Heat seared the backs of my eyes, pricking ferociously.

Crap.

I was going to start crying any second.

I was an angry crier. It was something I hated, but since I rarely got super angry, it wasn't something I thought about much.

But Rhodes made me absolutely furious.

I swallowed hard, blinking hard to keep the tears at bay as long as possible. "I get it, Rhodes. Okay? I freaking *get* it."

"Get *what*?" he hissed.

I looked away with a sniffle. Mortified that I was about to start crying in front of him, I barely managed to speak. "You don't like me ... like *that*. Fine, okay? I've accepted it. But you can't get mad when I try to move on."

"Larkin." His voice was so soft, so kind, it made me flinch.

I took a step back, swiping at the single tear that had escaped. "Don't, okay? I know this is my problem. You can't control how you feel any more than I can. But I miss my best friend, Rhodes. *That's* the worst part."

I blinked and more tears spilled down my cheeks.

I went to wipe them away, but Rhodes beat me there. His large hands, rough and calloused from years of working in the garage, came up to frame my face and raise my eyes so I had to look at him.

Like the independent woman I *wasn't*, I squeezed my eyes shut to avoid meeting his gaze.

He chuckled softly, a thumb smoothing over my cheek to catch the tear there. "Open your eyes, baby girl."

My body shook. My stomach took a steep dive.

I didn't want to look. I didn't want to see the pity in his eyes.

"You should go," I whispered, eyes still closed.

I needed him to leave so I could pick up all the pieces of my heart from the floor.

"Larkin, *look at me*," he ordered quietly.

Slowly, I lifted my lashes, blinking a few times to clear my blurry vision.

Sure enough, Rhodes was looking at me with nothing but kindness and softness.

He sighed softly. "I'm so sorry, Lark."

I gulped down a sob, the last shards of my broken heart crashing down around me. "It's fine. I'm fine."

His eyes drifted shut for just a second, agony twisting his features, before looking at me. "I'm sorry."

"You can't control how you feel," I whispered. He couldn't help *not* loving me any more than I could stop loving him.

"No," he agreed, his eyes searching mine. "You can't."

I put my hands over his wrists and gently pulled them away from my face. "It's okay, Rhodes."

I took a small step back and started to turn when his hands shot out and grabbed my waist, spinning me against the hard wall of his body.

"I'm sorry," he whispered once more before claiming my mouth with his.

5

LARKIN

I GASPED AS SOON AS HIS WARM MOUTH SLANTED OVER MINE, and that was the only sign he needed to invade and conquer.

And holy hell, did he ever conquer.

My hands clutched at his forearms as my legs threatened to give out. His tongue slid deliciously, sinfully, against mine. His kiss was slow and hungry, devouring and consuming.

I slid my arms up and around his neck, finally letting my hands tangle in his soft hair like I had wanted to do for years. My chest pressed to his, my soft curves yielding to his hard edges as I tried to get even closer.

His hands tightened around my waist, and he lifted me up in his arms like I was nothing. My legs wrapped around his back, locking at the ankles as he walked us several steps until my back hit the wall.

With a low groan that made an unfamiliar ache settle between my thighs, Rhodes deepened the kiss. One hand slid up my back, twisting around my loose hair until he had it wound around his fist. He tugged, breaking our kiss and arching my neck.

His teeth nipped at the exposed column of my throat, his tongue and lips soothing the bites. His mouth closed over a sensitive spot at the base of my neck I didn't even know existed, and I rocked my hips against his.

My breath caught, feeling the impressive and growing ridge in his jeans I could feel through my thin leggings.

I ground my hips against it a second before he pressed me harder into the wall, thrusting his hips into me.

"God," I choked out, my breaths ragged as the world spun around me.

His teeth nipped at my collar bone. Chest heaving, he pulled back, his eyes swirled with lust and desire.

"Tell me to stop," he ordered, licking his lips, his gaze dropping to my mouth.

I leaned forward, pressing my lips to his again. Need and want thrummed in my blood.

"No," I whispered against his mouth.

The world spun as he whirled us around. Still holding me, he walked out of the kitchen and into the family room, dropping me onto the sectional sofa. The soft cushions caught me as Rhodes stood over me, large and dominant and … whoa.

I swallowed, terrified to move.

He looked like he wanted to devour me whole.

Or run away as fast as he could.

I could see the war raging in his head as he looked at me. His jaw was tight, his eyes practically on fire as they swept my body.

"Don't go," I whispered, finally reaching a hand out to him.

Time suspended as I waited for him to make a decision that would shatter me one way or another.

He grabbed for my hand, but caught my wrist as he

lowered himself down, his weight pressing me harder into the cushions. I reached for him with my other hand, but his fingers quickly caught that one, too, lifting both arms over my head and transferring them into one of his hands, pinning them down.

His lips kicked up in a wicked grin, his free hand coming down my arm, smoothing across my face before slowly tracing down my chest, over my breast, my side, my hip.

His fingers curved into my thigh, lifting and wrapping my leg up around his waist, pressing us together.

I moaned, the sound low and breathy and foreign to me. I arched my back, but other than settling between my legs, he barely touched me.

I needed more.

His dark eyes swept up and down me, studying so intently I felt raw and exposed.

I tried tugging my arms down, but his grip was ironclad.

He arched a single brow. "Going somewhere?"

I huffed. "I want to touch you," I whispered, my words a desperate plea. I tried to wiggle my body, but he dropped the full weight of himself onto the lower part of my body.

I groaned at the added friction, but now I really couldn't move. He had immobilized me.

"Do you know," he started softly, dropping his mouth to my neck, peppering slow, burning kisses along the skin there, "how long I've waited for this?"

I squeezed my eyes shut, trying to focus on his words when every cell in my body was alive and being electrocuted. With each kiss, a new set of nerves came alive, sending off a cascade of sensations that rippled through me.

"What?" I finally managed.

His hand went to the hem of my shirt and dipped beneath, sliding up my ribcage. His mouth moved to my jaw.

"This," he repeated. "*Us*."

His lips found mine, but pulled away a second later.

I groaned at the loss, be he rewarded me with a roll of his hips that had stars bursting behind my eyes.

"Rhodes." My voice came out a breathy whimper that made him grin.

"God, I love how you say my name," he whispered before angling his mouth over mine. He timed the thrust of his tongue against mine with a snap of his hips until I was so turned on I wasn't sure if I was going to scream or cry.

Maybe both.

I struggled against his hold, needing to touch him. To my utter frustration, he completely froze. He lifted his hips from mine, his head coming up so I couldn't reach his lips.

"Rhodes," I whined, trying to wiggle my hips in encouragement. He was a guy, right? Wasn't this a thing guys usually just went for without hesitation?

His free hand stilled my hips, holding me in place.

"You done?" he asked calmly, like he was asking what I got on my math test.

"I'm *trying* to be," I snapped, letting my head flop back with a groan.

He chuckled low in his throat, the sound making my toes curl. His dark eyes swept my body, lingering on my lips, the swell of my breasts, the place between my thighs I desperately needed some sort of pressure against.

The thumb of the hand holding mine gently rubbed a soothing circle on the inside of my wrist.

"Please," I begged.

He lowered his lips slowly to mine, his kiss sweet and

wet and hot as he explored. He lifted his head after a second and glanced up at our hands before giving me his eyes.

He sighed deeply, rolling his eyes playfully. "You're ruining my fun, baby girl."

He slowly released me and sat back onto his knees.

I barely had a second to mourn the loss of his weight on my body before his hands were sliding up, taking my sweater with them. When he got to my bra, he hesitated, his eyes going to mine.

I finished the job for him, taking my sweater off the rest of the way and sending it sailing across the room. I lay back, watching as his eyes drank me in.

Part of me realized I should feel embarrassed or *something*, but watching the way his eyes darkened with lust, all I felt was a feminine smugness. His attention was locked on me, following the rise and fall of my chest with each breath I took.

I couldn't help the grin that curved on my lips knowing he liked what he saw.

I glanced down and inwardly winced, wishing when I changed my jeans I had opted for something other than a virginal white cotton bra with scalloped lace trim.

Then again, Rhodes didn't seem to mind that I just barely filled out my B-cups.

He traced the edges of the scallops with a single finger, his expression reverent as his eyes followed every dip and curve. I was holding my breath, every cell in my body alive and firing and poised on the edge of something incredible.

His dark eyes flicked up to mine as his finger landed on the front clasp of my bra. His eyes were absolutely blazing.

"Tell me to stop," he repeated, his voice huskier and

rougher than before. I felt the finger pressed in the valley between my breasts tremble for just a second.

I held his gaze with mine. "Don't you dare stop."

Any last traces of hesitation melted away, replaced with something hot and needy. He deftly undid the clasp and the cups of my bra fell away, exposing me. His hand slid over one mound, cupping it, testing its weight in his hand.

I arched into his touch, wanting more. Needing more. My hands curled in his shirt, trying to pull him down.

He pulled his hand away quickly, fixing me with a reproving look that had me flushing for an entirely new reason.

"Rhodes—"

"Hands above your head," he told me. Demanded of me.

Swallowing, I did as he said. I clasped my hands together, stretched above my head.

He hummed in approval and moved a hand back to my breast, slowly kneading the flesh around my nipple. Every time his fingers got closer to the tight peak, they ghosted away. After he did this for a fourth time, I voiced my protest with a frustrated cry.

Which made him *smirk*.

I huffed. "Dammit, Rhodes—"

He suddenly lowered his mouth, closing it over one tip and sucking deeply.

"Shit," I hissed, almost reaching for him as my back arched up. I remembered my hands at the last second and put them back over my head, fisting them in a throw pillow I found tucked into the corner of the cushions.

"Good girl," he praised, turning his attention to the other breast, his teeth scraping the tender skin there before he laid his tongue against it, drawing it between his lips and kissing it as thoroughly as he had kissed my mouth.

My body was going to combust. I was going to explode into a million tiny pieces.

The hand he had kept at my hip started to move then, first skirting the waistband of my leggings. Boldly, he reached down and cupped me between my legs.

I gasped, my eyes going wide at the sudden feel of him touching me there. A surge of wetness slicked the skin between my thighs, and I briefly wondered if he could tell I was completely soaked.

A low growl of approval rumbled deep in his chest as he lifted his head from my breast, his eyes going to where his hand gently, but firmly, held me.

It took absolutely everything in my not to move my hips, not to try and find some sort of relief from the pressure building in me. I was ready to detonate like an atom bomb.

He looked up at me through a fringe of dark lashes, a lock of hair falling in his eyes. The look he gave me was a complete cross between an adorable boy next door and a hot, sexy bad boy. His fingers curled against my center.

A shiver tripped up my spine as I sucked in a shuddering breath.

The corner of one side of his mouth hitched up in a gorgeous grin. "Still with me?"

I nodded quickly.

His hand relaxed. "Words, Larkin. I need to hear the words."

"I'm with you," I whispered in a rush. "Don't stop. *Please*, don't stop."

He gave me a dazzling, brilliant smile that was all

Rhodes. He slid his hand into the front of my leggings, into the front of my panties.

The first touch of the calloused pad of his finger against the taut bundle of nerves nearly made me scream. The sensation was overloading me. Every nerve ending short circuited and fired to life at the same time.

His fingers glided easily between my legs, the wetness that had been gathering since he first kissed me making it easy for him to ease a finger inside of me.

I hissed a sharp breath, not sure if I liked this feeling, this invasion. The pressure was strange and new. Not painful, but not exactly comfortable either.

He waited, gauging my reaction, his eyes missing nothing. His thumb gently smoothed down the side of my clit, making my hips jerk. Like pieces of a puzzle clicking together, that fullness I felt from him inside me combined with that simply touch had my body understanding why people made such a big deal out of sex and how good it felt.

I blew out a long, shuddering breath, my eyes damn near rolling back in my head.

His thumb stroked the other side, his finger hooking slightly inside of me.

"Oh, God," I choked out, white knuckling the pillow. "Rhodes."

He slowly pulled his finger out, then thrust it back in as his thumb started rubbing lazy circles around my clit. My head started to spin.

"Touch me."

He barely finished the command before I let the pillow go, my arms coming around him and tangling in his long hair. I pulled his mouth down to mine desperately, our teeth clicking together as I arced up, pressing myself harder against his hand.

His tongue invaded my mouth thoroughly as he tucked a second finger into me, his thumb never giving up the deliberate, torturously slow circling of my clit.

He kept part of his weight braced on his free arm so as not to crush me, but I pulled at him harder until he surrendered, falling half on top of me.

"Come on, Lark," he murmured against my lips. "Come for me."

He curled his fingers inside of me, hitting a spot that had the world going white around me while his thumb pressed more intently against my clit.

I rocked my hips into his hand once. Twice.

The third time, my body came apart, a ragged cry falling from my lips as Rhodes kept pumping his fingers in and out, dragging out my orgasm. My entire body convulsed around him, every muscle clenched tight as I rode out the wave. I shuddered through the aftershock ripples, his hand slowing, easing my body down back to earth.

His mouth crashed down onto mine again, his fingers still inside me, not moving, as he kissed me slowly, languidly. My arms felt heavy around his neck, my body sinking deeper into the cushions.

Rhodes pulled away slowly, sliding his fingers out of my body and then out of my pants. To my utter shock, he lifted his fingers to his mouth and licked them clean. My empty core clenched at the insanely hot visual.

"You taste incredible," he murmured, something dark and unreadable in his gaze that had my body struggling to come alive again.

"Rhodes," I started slowly, trying to sit up. Reality was starting to sink in.

Rhodes reached behind me, pulling a blanket off the back of the couch and wrapping it around us both. He tucked me against the back of the couch, stretching out beside me and pulling me into his arms.

"We'll talk in the morning, Larkin," he said softly, his lips pressing against my forehead.

I could still feel how aroused he was, the hard length of him pressed against my hip. "But-"

He kissed me softly, gently. "Sleep, now. We'll talk this all out tomorrow."

My eyes were already drooping. "Promise?"

His warm breath fanned over my face. "Promise."

6
RHODES

I WAS GOING TO HELL.

Looking over at where Larkin was sound asleep on the couch, I leaned against the wall by the window looking out over the backyard.

It had finally stopped snowing, but there was a solid two and a half feet of snow out there. Probably more where it had drifted.

I looked back at Larkin, the bright moonlight slanting through the windows over her body. She was curled up in a ball under the blanket, her hands tucked under her chin.

God, she was so beautiful it hurt to look at her.

I knew the second I kissed her I had fucked things up. Probably for good because there was absolutely no way to go back from this.

There was no way in hell I would ever see her as my best friend, Larkin.

Watching her come against my hand, feeling the way her body trembled and surrendered completely to me? There was no way I could unsee that.

Hell, it had been four hours and my dick was just now starting to settle down. I finally got up off the couch because every little sigh she made in her sleep had me almost reaching for her to finish what I had started.

I had pulled myself up, cleaned up the mess from dinner and then paced the floor for a few minutes before settling in to watch her sleep. She looked so sweet and innocent asleep, a big difference from the girl who a few hours earlier was riding my hand.

I blew out a long breath, trying to get a grip.

Larkin wasn't ready for sex yet. And I wasn't ready for sex with Larkin yet, despite what my body thought.

I meant what I had said—she and I needed to sit down and talk all of this out in the morning. There was a lot she needed to know. A lot I needed to say. I wasn't exactly looking forward to it, but we needed to make sure we were on the same page.

Or, I needed to make sure she was on my page. Because there was no way I was going back. I was too selfish, too much of an asshole.

The second I tasted her in that first kiss, she was mine. She would always be mine.

For the first time in a long time, I wished I had someone to talk to about this. Someone like my father who could give me insight and advice.

Sure, I had Remy. Remy was an amazing best friend, but he was just starting to figure out his own thing with Skye. I wanted someone who had been there. Gabe was an option, but …

He wasn't my dad.

I dropped my head back against the wall with a thump.

A sharp gasp had me looking over to see Larkin sit up, clutching a hand to the top of the blanket around her chest.

"Rhodes?"

I stepped out of the shadows, feeling like an asshole. She thought I had left.

Which I probably should have, but I was fucking gone for this girl.

"I'm still here," I said softly, moving across the room and sitting on the edge of the couch beside her. I brushed some of her hair out of her eyes, letting my fingers trace the curve of her cheek, map the contour of her lips.

Her big brown eyes were huge as she searched my face. "I thought you might have ... gone home."

There was something so sad, so accepting in her tone, that I physically flinched.

I cupped the side of her face. "I told you we had some things to talk about in the morning. I'm not going anywhere, Lark."

She sagged in relief, letting her eyes drift shut for a second as she relaxed into my touch. "Good. I don't like it when you leave."

That small admission, spoken in such a tiny voice, absolutely wrecked me.

She looked around my shoulder, giving me a slight smile. "It's after midnight."

I glanced back at the clock on the cable box. "Yeah."

Her smile widened. "It's morning. Technically."

I couldn't help but laugh. "You should sleep."

"So should *you*," she replied, sitting up and tucking the blanket around her where I wished it would fall down. "But since we're both up, maybe we should ... talk?"

I opened my mouth, but a sharp knock on the door cut me off.

I got to my feet, glancing down at Larkin. "You expecting a delivery?"

She shot to her feet, eyes wide. "Who the hell could that be? There's like three feet of snow outside."

I grabbed her arm to stop her. "Lark, maybe you put a shirt on before you answer the door?"

She blushed and laughed, awkwardly clutching the blanket over her chest. "Um, right."

I waited, but she didn't move.

"Can you turn around?" she asked, her cheeks a bright shade of red.

I cocked my head to the side, amused as hell. "You realize I've seen all of this before, right? In vivid, high definition detail. I can tell you how many freckles you have on your—"

She slapped a hand over my mouth. "Oh, my God, Rhodes. Seriously?"

I smirked under her fingers before darting my tongue out and licking her.

"Ew!" she laughed, twisting away and nearly tripping over the blanket.

With a loud, exasperated sigh, and to my utter delight, she dropped the blanket, setting her hands on her hips. "Happy?"

My gaze instantly dropped to her breasts, greedily drinking in the soft swells and the dusty pink tips.

Another, more insistent, knock sounded.

I growled, my wolf as pissed as I was at the interruption.

"I'll be happy when whoever the hell it is goes away," I muttered darkly, heading for the door.

"Rhodes—I can answer the door!"

I was already in the hall, wrenching the door open. My eyes locked on one set of eyes, then the identical pair of the guys in front of me.

"What the hell are you doing here?" I demanded, glaring at one McAllister twin and then the other.

Kyle's gaze narrowed. "We could ask you the same question."

"Where's Larkin?" Konnor demanded, trying to look past me.

"Getting dressed," I replied with a smirk as I leaned against the doorframe. I shook my hair out of my eyes.

Kyle winced, but what I said only seemed to piss Konnor off.

"Again," I said, louder, wanting to get back to the half naked girl in the other room, "what the hell are you doing here?"

"Kyle? Konnor?" Larkin came up behind me, wrapping her arms around herself as the cold seeped into the room. I glanced back at her, thankful as hell she remembered to put her bra back on in addition to her sweater.

But her hair was loose around her face, hanging in long waves, her eyes still sleepy. I hated that these two asshats were seeing her like this.

Only I should see how she looked after she had just woken up hours after crashing from the biggest orgasm of her damn life.

"We texted you," Kyle said, his voice low like I couldn't hear him right in front of my face.

"We wanted to make sure you were okay," Konnor added.

"Since your parents are gone," Kyle finished.

I blinked slowly. Jesus, these two even talked in tandem. Like they shared a single brain.

Larkin coughed into her hand, her eyes flicking to me for a second before looking back at them. She ducked her head guiltily. "Guys—"

"She's fine," I cut in sharply, hating she felt any sort of regret for what happened between us. "It's late and it's cold. Maybe we could do this at a time that *isn't* midnight?"

Konnor glared at me. "We were talking to Larkin, Rhodes. Not you."

"And now you're saying goodnight," I retorted, standing up straight with a warning growl.

Maybe Konnor needed a reminder of his place in the pack, and in Larkin's life.

"Rhodes!" Larkin gasped, her small hand grabbing the back of my shirt. "Chill out."

"I'm not entirely sure why you're at *our* girlfriend's house," Konnor kept going, "but we've got it from here."

My entire body went rigid as his words registered. Ice settled in my veins that had nothing to do with the weather. My anger flared, waking my wolf.

"Excuse me?" I asked quietly.

"Okay, guys, seriously," Larkin protested, coming around in front of me. "We're not doing this."

"We really just came to check on you," Kyle said quickly, his blue eyes searching hers in a way that made me want to yank them out of their sockets. "We were worried about you."

"Thank you, Kyle, but—"

"But I guess we shouldn't be shocked to find Rhodes here," Konnor continued, holding my gaze in an open challenge that had me snarling. "Even in a blizzard he has to find some girl to try and screw. Even if she is already claimed by another."

Larkin sucked in a sharp breath, bristling beside me. Even Kyle looked a little unsure now.

"But since when has that stopped Rhodes? He doesn't do much except think with his dick," Konnor spat. His furious gaze turned to Larkin. "But I'm pretty disappointed you bought his act, Larkin."

I barely registered Larkin yelling before my fist slammed into his mouth, knocking him back several feet. He lost his balance and tumbled down the steps of the porch, falling into the snow. It would have been pretty damn funny if I wasn't ready to rip his head off.

I glanced at Kyle, but his gaze was already down at the ground. He had always been the more submissive twin, which was the only reason he wasn't joining his brother in the snow.

Konnor came up, spitting a mouthful of blood into the snow.

"Rhodes!" Larkin yanked at my arm.

"I'm only saying this once," I said through gritted teeth, barely keeping a tether on my wolf. "Larkin isn't yours."

Kyle slunk back a step while Konnor had the nerve to bare his teeth at me.

I smiled, ready to throw down. Sex and violence were two sides of the same coin, and since sex wasn't currently an option, violence would suffice.

"You guys need to leave," Larkin said, her voice quiet but firm. "I appreciate you coming to check on me, but I'm fine." She hesitated before touching my arm, leaning against my side. "*We're* fine."

Konnor looked ready to argue, but Kyle was already going down the steps, pulling his brother back. He looked apologetically at Larkin.

"I'm sorry," he said sincerely to her, not looking at me. "We'll see you around."

Konnor spit out one last mouthful of blood and stalked off, at least as much as he could in several feet of snow. I watched, arms folded across my chest, until they rounded the corner of the street.

Larkin gave me a small shove from behind. "What the *hell* was that, Rhodes?"

I turned slowly, still feeding off the rage from my wolf. It was Larkin, which I knew, but we both interpreted the shove as a challenge.

But with Larkin it was less about violence, and more about working out my aggression in other ways.

She swallowed and took a step back. "Don't look at me like that."

"Then don't touch me like that," I countered.

With a huff, she retreated back into the house, but left the door open for me as she did. I went back inside after her, shutting and locking the door.

I wasn't surprised when I found her standing in the middle of the living room, hands on her hips, waiting for me.

"Well?"

"Well, what?" I asked, coming into the room.

"I cannot *believe* you," she seethed, raking a hand through her long hair. It spilled across her shoulders like a silk curtain I couldn't wait to fist in my hands again.

"I'm sorry," I replied drolly, "I guess I have an issue with two guys showing up, claiming to be your *boyfriends* after you spent the evening riding *my* hand."

Her mouth dropped open. "They're not my boyfriends!"

"Do *they* know that?" I asked, trying to stay calm when I

spoke. All I could see was that fucking kiss at Christmas. Every time they were around Larkin at GPA.

"One date, Rhodes," she snapped, holding up a single finger. "We went on *one* stupid date."

"Wait—you went out with them?" Jealousy snaked around my gut. I was going to be sick.

She sighed. "Yes. The other night. When you were cleaning up."

Hurt flashed through me, the sting bitter. "And you didn't tell me?"

She spread her arms wide at her sides. "It's not like you and I talk much anymore, Rhodes. The last twenty-four hours is the most we've talked all year!"

I scoffed. "That's not true."

"Yes, it—" She cut herself off with a frustrated groan. "You know what? It doesn't matter. I'm allowed to date, Rhodes. You made it pretty damn clear you wanted *nothing* to do with me."

I crossed the room and was in front of her in a flash, reaching out and hauling her against my body. "Does this feel like I want nothing to do with you?" I pressed my cock against her. The damn hard-on hadn't quit since earlier. Now it was at full attention, loving the fight and fire in her.

Larkin gasped softly, her hands coming up to grab my shirt for balance as she tipped her head back to look at me.

"How was I supposed to know that days ago?" she finally asked, her tone softer. "Days ago, when you were still giving me the silent treatment. The same way you've acted for the last *year*."

"I know I've been an asshole," I admitted, my hands going tight around her hips. "I know I have a lot to apologize for. But I'm not going to apologize for what happened out there. Konnor was out of line."

"Yeah, he was," she agreed. "I'm sorry he interpreted one date—"

"And a kiss," I muttered darkly.

Her brows lifted. "You know about that?"

"I *saw* that," I replied stiffly, looking away. "I left right after it happened."

"Why?" she pressed softly, one hand sliding up my chest and winding around my neck.

Now or never.

"Because it wasn't *me* you were kissing," I answered honestly. "Because it should have been me."

Her eyes went soft, her lips curving into a gorgeous smile that stole my breath.

"You're right. It should have been you." Her other arm came up around my neck, pulling me close. "It's always been *you*."

7

RHODES

WAKING UP WITH LARKIN WAS LIKE REALIZING YOU WERE IN A dream that didn't end. It was amazing and surreal.

But Larkin was definitely a bed hog.

We had started in the middle of her double bed – she definitely needed a bigger bed – but now my ass was practically hanging off the edge and she was all but completely on top of me, her head resting against my chest, her hand splayed dangerously low on my stomach.

I was glad I had taken off my shirt before we slipped into her bed since my girl was a miniature furnace.

I wasn't as glad she opted to put *on* a shirt before going to bed.

I stroked the back of her hand, marveling at the soft skin, how much smaller her fingers were than mine.

I had screwed plenty of girls in my life, but I hadn't ever slept with one. Larkin was my first.

I wasn't an asshole. Not completely. I had never kicked a girl out of my bed, but if she crashed there, I just crashed …

elsewhere. Sleeping with someone felt too intimate, too intense.

Looking down at Larkin, watching the way her dark lashes fanned out across the soft swell of her cheek, the way her heart shaped mouth was softly parted as she breathed, I knew I wasn't wrong.

There was something sacred in this moment.

"Oh, God," she muttered, turning her face into my shoulder with a groan. "It's so freaking early. Turn the damn sun down."

Like I said, sacred.

Chuckling, I kissed the top of her head.

Her body went stiff on top of mine and she slowly lifted her head from my chest, her eyes round and wide.

"Hey," I said softly, tucking a lock of tangled dark hair behind her ear.

"I didn't dream this?" she whispered, her eyes searching mine.

"You didn't dream this," I assured her.

She didn't look convinced. "Are you sure? Because this is a lot like the dream I had last week. And the week before that. And basically multiple times every week for the last five years."

I rolled her onto her back, pressing her into the mattress, my lips kissing the delicate skin of her neck.

"Not."

I kissed her jaw.

"A."

Her cheek.

"Dream."

Her lips.

Her mouth immediately opened for me, welcoming me, her arms looping around my shoulders and pulling me closer.

"Still feels like a dream," she murmured against my mouth, smiling.

"A good dream?"

Her eyes opened. "The best dream."

I tried not to grind against her, but it was morning and she was radiating serious heat from where her hips cradled me between her legs. I could definitely get used to waking up like this.

She made a sudden face, her nose wrinkling. "I have to pee."

Dropping my head to her shoulder, I laughed loudly, my shoulders shaking.

She pushed me off, and swung her legs over the side of the bed. Watching her walk away from the bed, her ass in a tiny pair of shorts, I could no longer blame my rock hard dick on it being morning.

Minutes later she was coming out of the bathroom, hesitating in the doorway, her expression worried.

"What's up?" I propped myself up on my elbows, waiting for her to come to me.

She meandered to the edge of the bed, climbing up and sitting on her knees facing me.

"It's morning."

"I'm aware," I remarked, not sure where she was going.

She twisted her hands in the fluffy pink comforter we had been wrapped in. "Do you still want to talk? About … us?"

I sat up, making sure I had her eyes before speaking. "Absolutely."

Her shoulders dropped with relief, a smile breaking across her face. "Good."

I reached for her, tangling my fingers in hers. "We definitely need to talk. And we're definitely *going* to talk. Why don't I run back to my house and take a shower?"

She nodded, her smile tight. "Yeah. Shower definitely sounds ... good."

Something in her tone made me pause. "You okay?"

A soft flush started at her neck, working its way up her cheeks. "I'm a little ... sore."

I wasn't sure if I wanted to smirk or slap myself.

But it helped me remember that I definitely needed to take things at Larkin's speed.

"But that's normal, right?" she asked quickly. She waved it off. "Ignore me."

I snorted. Ignoring Larkin wasn't an option.

I tugged on her hand until she fell forward, crashing into my chest. I kissed her quickly. "What happened last night? We don't have to do anything you're not ready for."

She reared back, her eyebrows flying towards her hairline. "Who said I wasn't ready?"

I frowned. "You said—"

"That I was a little sore, yeah," she muttered, ducking her head. "But we're definitely doing *that* again ... right?"

I chuckled, unable to keep my hands off of her. "Whatever you want, Lark."

She lifted her eyes to mine. "And if I want ... more?"

I swallowed, my throat suddenly dry, trying to remind myself which head was in charge here as all blood rushed south. "We can talk about that, too."

"Okay," she agreed with an easy smile. She kissed me quickly, pulling away just as fast. "I'll meet you at your house? After you shower? That way you can work on the motorcycle this afternoon if you want?"

I tried not to smirk. That wasn't the engine I was hoping to have purring in my hands this afternoon, but sure.

☪

Larkin

It took what felt like forever to take a shower, dry my hair and get dressed. It also might have been because I spent an insane amount of time trying to figure out what set of underwear to put on and then adding a few coats of mascara to my eyes.

And maybe a flavored lip balm.

I drew the line at curling my hair.

I texted my mom, letting her know I was fine so my parents wouldn't worry. They weren't due to come home for another couple of days, so hopefully the roads would be cleared by then.

I packed an extra set of clothes to change into after trudging through the snow, but I realized I didn't need them as I walked outside and saw Rhodes had shoveled a path between our houses.

I smiled at the thoughtful touch and started walking across the yards. His front door was unlocked when I went inside, and I could hear his shower running in the bathroom on the second floor.

A braver girl might have gone up to the shower and joined him.

But I wasn't quite that brave yet, especially before coffee … which I smelled coming from the kitchen.

I dropped my bag of clothes by the door and toed off my shoes, wandering through the living room on my way to the kitchen, marveling at the change.

Rhodes had clearly spent time cleaning. His dad definitely wasn't big on cleanliness, and every time I had come over when we were kids, I could tell it bothered Rhodes.

It bothered him enough that I knew his room here and at GPA was white-glove inspection ready. Even the garage, which was notoriously dirty by nature, was always organized and clean, the scent of lingering diesel fuel the only hint that he often spent days elbows deep in oil and grease.

I knew his kitchen almost as well as I knew my own. I walked in and poured myself a cup of coffee from the pot he had brewed into the mug he had set out for me.

I tried to ignore the pang of my heart at how sweet he was. Instead, I made myself a cup of liquid energy and started pulling ingredients out to make a few quick omelets. I was just plating them when Rhodes came downstairs, padding into the kitchen in bare feet, jeans, and a t-shirt that said "No Pants Are The Best Pants".

I snorted, shaking my head.

He wasn't wrong.

His arms came around my waist as I set the second plate on the table, pulling my back against his front. Taking a deep breath, I inhaled the scent of soap and Rhodes.

I needed to bottle this scent and carry it around.

Waking up with him this morning, I had quickly realized why Skye needed Remy to stay the night.

My sleep had been dreamless, and the best I'd had since my parents left.

I wasn't stupid enough to think that having a guy next to me was a fix for the nightmares that sometimes crept in. But not being alone helped.

Rhodes made me feel safe, awake or asleep.

His lips found the curve of my neck, gently nipping and

suckling at the tender flesh there until I shivered. I felt his smile against my skin.

"This smells amazing," he murmured, sweeping my hair to the side for better access.

I tried not to squirm. "It's just eggs."

He gave a soft hum, his teeth sinking into my neck for just a second. The quick flash of pain created a sudden tug between my thighs that had me gasping.

"I wasn't talking about the food, baby girl," he said, his hands squeezing my waist.

My stomach trembled at the term of endearment. Rhodes had actually called me that before, adopting the nickname since I was a year younger than him and our friends. But he had never said it with so much heat behind it as his mouth moved across my neck.

Another delicious shiver wriggled down my spine.

He chuckled, his breath warm. "We should eat. Then talk."

Logically I knew he was right, but the second he pulled away, I was fighting the urge to reach for him. Now that I finally had him, now that we were finally *together*, I was terrified of letting him get too far away. Like the dandelion fluff we made wishes on in the summer.

One strong blow and it would all be over.

We ate in relative silence. I tried eating fast, but the more I chewed, the more the food settled like bricks in my stomach. I kept sneaking glances, but Rhodes didn't seem phased by anything. If he had the same worries I did, he was keeping them locked down.

After watching me push the last half of my omelet around the plate for several minutes, he finally got up.

"Let's go."

He held a hand out for me, but it took me a second to accept it. A small frown deepened on his face as he noted my hesitation.

He pulled me into the living room, sitting on the couch. I went to sit beside him, but he surprised me by yanking me down onto his lap.

With a startled yelp, I fell on top of him, barely catching myself on his massive shoulders before I completely toppled over. My knees went on either side of him so I was straddling his lap. I went to adjust my position to something less intimate, but his hands came down on my hips, holding me still.

"Don't move," he said softly, his eyes drinking me in.

"Rhodes—" This felt too intense, too intimate.

He never stopped looking at me. "We're having this talk, and I want to see your eyes the whole time. No more secrets. No more hiding, Lark."

I slowly nodded, letting the lower half of my body relax onto his strong thighs. I dropped my hands from his chest to his wrists, letting him study me.

"I need the truth," he started quietly, never breaking eye contact. The submissive wolf in me wanted to yield, to look away from him, but I knew he wanted me to keep his gaze. Rhodes might have been my best friend, and slowly was becoming more, but he was still a beta. Still someone with a high rank in our pack that deserved, demanded, deference.

"Kyle and Konnor," he went on, and I sucked in a sharp breath, not expecting that.

His thumb stroked over the curve of my hip. "If you want to be with them, I'll step aside. I just want you to be happy."

"I don't!" I blurted the words out as fast as I could, nearly stumbling on the simple syllables. I shook my head vehemently. "I don't."

A ghost of a smile flitted across his face. "Lark, all I'm saying is that if you have feelings for them, I understand. We can stop this … now. Go back to how things were before."

Before?

My mind couldn't wrap around that word.

Before, when we barely talked? Before, when it felt like I was being stabbed every time I saw him with a girl? Before, when I let two guys kiss me under some stupid mistletoe and felt sick about it the entire time?

An oily, insidious thought came to me. "Do you *want* me to say yes?"

He blinked. "What?"

I swallowed hard, terrified to ask. "Do you want me to say that I would rather be with them? To give you an out?"

His eyes drifted shut. "Lark—"

"If that's what you want, then just say it, Rhodes," I spat, fury rising. On its heels was the realization that I would never survive this. There was no going back to before for me. Not after last night.

"Larkin, I'm *not* saying that," he told me firmly, his dark eyes flashing. "Last night wasn't some random hook up. But I also know I've been an asshole this last year, so I can't blame you if you wanted something less complicated."

I sighed. "No, Rhodes. I don't want them. I've spent the last few months trying to prove to myself that I could move on from you. That's all that was." I shook my head. "I did a pretty crappy job at it, too."

"So no Kyle, no Konnor?"

"Only you," I breathed, loving the way his entire expression shifted to a strange mix of hunger and peace at the same time.

"Only you," he echoed.

I arched a brow. "That's going to seriously curb your harem."

"Harem?" he repeated, brows raising dramatically. His hands tightened on me.

I let him go, wrapping my arms around my waist, feeling stupidly jealous and angry at all the girls I had seen come and go the last couple of years both at school and in the pack.

"I don't have a harem," he told me uneasily.

Now I snorted. "Right. The endless parade of women the last few years?"

"Larkin—"

"I get it, okay?" I cut him off, trying to be mature even if just thinking about it left a rancid taste in my mouth. "We weren't together. You're allowed to … do whatever you want. Or, I guess, *whoever* you want."

I flinched at the bitterness in my voice. I sounded like I was whining or harping or some other annoying verb.

He was quiet for several beats.

"I'm sorry," I apologized. "That came out a lot more judgemental than I wanted."

"Truth is, I lost track of how many girls, women, I've slept with," he admitted quietly, shame coloring his tone. "But every single time I was with them, I only saw one face. In my mind, I was only ever with one person. Each one started as a distraction, but it all ended the same way."

I held my breath, eyes huge.

"You," he whispered. "I only ever saw you."

8

RHODES

"I ONLY EVER SAW YOU," I ADMITTED.

I knew it made me the world's biggest douche, admitting that while I may have fucked dozens of girls, women, in the last few years, I did it picturing her face every single time.

Every. Single. Time.

It got to the point when I could only finish if I closed my eyes and saw her face.

I had never told anyone that, not even Remy, who knew more shit about me than I sometimes knew about myself.

It wasn't fair to the girls I had been with, but they never knew. At least, I hoped they didn't.

Larkin's soft hands came up, framing my face as her eyes desperately searched mine. "Why didn't you ever tell me?"

Now it was my turn to swallow hard. The lump in my throat seemed impossibly massive as I tried to form words around it.

"Because I knew you deserved better than me."

I exhaled slowly, that final admission both a weight off my shoulders and an anchor around my neck.

She reared back, eyes wide. "What?"

"You deserve better than me, Larkin," I repeated. "Baby girl, look at us. You're so fucking smart, Lark. You're going to college, you have amazing parents. You're going to have an incredible life. And look at me." I shook my head. "My mom left. My dad is a drunk who couldn't handle that."

"I *am* looking at you," she replied softly, fiercely. Her eyes practically glowed. "You're the guy who I can always count on. My best friend. The guy who told me I could absolutely handle extra classes to graduate. The same guy who helped me splint a bunny's broken foot in the backyard when I was twelve."

I couldn't help but chuckle at that. I remembered all too well a twelve year old Larkin sobbing in her backyard about a bunny who would never find his family again because he had a broken foot. I had been thirteen, and about to go out to the quarry with Remy and a bunch of other guys, but instead I stayed back and helped her bandage up the terrified animal and take it into town to the vet.

I never had the heart to tell her we probably scared the rabbit half to death since all it could smell on us was our wolf scent.

She traced my brows. "If my life is going to be incredible, it's because you're in it, too. Why can't you see how amazing you are?"

I suddenly regretted having her sit on my lap, because there was no escaping her gaze. The way she saw me.

"It's not just that," I continued. "Lark, my dad lost it when my mom left. He *lost* it. And I used to think he was the biggest pussy in the world for that. I hated him so much, for so long because I didn't get why he couldn't pull it together."

Sighing, I dropped my head back against the couch. "But

the idea of you ever walking away or leaving … I get it. I don't think I could take losing you. And I feel like I'll always want to hold some part of me back to protect myself. Baby, you deserve a guy who will give you everything. Not almost everything."

"Okay, first of all," she started, adjusting on my lap so she was above me, and I had to look up at her fierce beauty, "I am *not* your mother. I don't know what the hell her problem was, but I would never walk away from you. And you are *not* your father. You would never do what he did, Rhodes."

Her words soothed the jagged edges of a wound I had left gaping and festering for years, but it was still there. The scars still ran deep.

I knew logically that Larkin wasn't my mother. Even if she woke up one day and realized I wasn't good enough for her, no way would she leave her kid behind.

Shit.

My heart seized in my chest at the thought of her kid.

Our kid.

The thought made me lightheaded, but God, I wanted that.

"Why now?" she asked softly, biting her lower lip and worrying it between her teeth. "What changed?"

Everything.

I cleared my throat. "Seeing you at Christmas with … those guys, kissing them. Fuck, I don't know, Larkin. It made me so angry and so sad. I've tried everything I could think of to stay away from you this year, but you're always *there*."

"Sorry about that?" she said, narrowing her eyes.

I huffed, smoothing her hair back from her face, holding her still to look me in the eye. "All I've ever wanted it is to be with you."

Her eyes went soft.

"But I knew you deserved someone who could give you everything, and I didn't think I was that guy," I added. "But I want to try to be. For you. For us."

She leaned forward and kissed me, her lips gentle against mine.

"I'll probably mess this up at some point," I warned her when she pulled back.

She shrugged. "Me, too. It's not like I have a lot of practice with dating or ... other stuff." Her blush was adorable.

"We don't have to do *other stuff*," I reminded her, even if my body was seriously not on board with that option.

Larkin was worth whatever wait.

Her eyes narrowed. "I thought I said I didn't want to wait."

My laugh was sudden and loud. This girl was seriously going to kill me.

"Okay," I replied, smiling.

"We just need to *talk*," she added. "If you start feeling like you're messing up or having doubts, tell me and I'll remind you how awesome you are. But don't shut me out again, Rhodes. I hate when you do that."

Swallowing, I nodded, pulling her down for a hug. "Deal."

She cuddled against my chest, and I could have stayed like that the rest of the day, but she sat up after a few minutes, her eyes serious.

"Are we ... telling people about this? About us?"

My stomach dipped. "We don't have to if you don't want to."

Her mouth dropped open in shock. "That's not what I meant at all. I know you don't usually do girlfriends—"

"I don't have girlfriends," I told her firmly, cutting her off. Her mouth snapped shut.

I raised a hand, cradling her jaw, feeling her pulse thrumming like a hummingbird taking flight. "But you're not just a girlfriend, Larkin."

"What am I?" she asked softly.

My lips curved into a smile. "Mine." I sat up, pulling her down until my lips were almost on hers. "And you can bet your sweet ass I'm telling the entire fucking world you belong to me."

I devoured her mouth hungrily, demanding entrance, my tongue sweeping into her mouth with raw possessiveness.

My wolf rumbled in approval.

She was ours.

Larkin gasped into my mouth, her small fists grabbing onto my shoulders as I rolled her until her back was pressed into the cushions of the couch and I was on top.

I kissed her slowly, taking my time to explore every part of her mouth. What made her gasp, what made her moan, what made her hips rock into me. I ignored when she wrapped a leg around the small of my back, trying to press me against her center.

I smirked against her lips at her frustrated groan.

"Rhodes, *please*," she whimpered, her begging doing all sorts of things to my body.

"Please what?" I asked, catching her bottom lip between my teeth and tugging. I smoothed a hand down her side, barely touching the swell of her breast even as she arched up to find my fingers.

"Stop teasing," she muttered, hands tangling in my hair to pull me down.

"Then tell me what you want," I murmured, wanting to

hear the words from her mouth. Wanting to hear the desperate need in her tone.

"You," she gasped, as I finally rolled my hips to hers.

"You have me," I replied, lifting off of her once again. Her hips chased after mine, but I stayed them with a firm hand to her abdomen. "I'm right here, baby."

She growled. "*Touch* me."

I smiled against her neck, nipping her collar bone. "I *am* touching you."

"You know what I mean!" she snapped, hands fisting against my scalp.

I pulled back, looking down at her. "No, I don't."

Lie. But I needed to hear her say. I wanted to hear her breathless and begging.

"Tell me where you want me to touch you."

Her cheeks flushed, but her eyes glittered with desire and frustration.

I arched a brow, waiting for her.

Larkin didn't break eye contact as she reached for my hand, moving it until I was pressed against her center. Jesus, the amount of heat coming off of her was a palpable thing. I could scent her arousal, and I knew she would be wet when I touched her.

"*Here*," she said, her voice breaking when I pressed my fingers firmly against her leggings.

Yup, totally soaked.

Before I could overthink it, I slid off her body, dropping to my knees on the floor beside her. I pulled her hips down to the edge of the couch, hooking my fingers in the sides of her leggings. I looked up at her, checking to see if she was with me.

Larkin bit her lower lip, the sight of her teeth catching the flesh I had worked over and made plump and red making my dick even harder against my jeans.

Fuck, I needed to get control of myself.

"I've never …" She coughed a little, the embarrassed flush returning.

"Me neither," I admitted softly, my eyes lifting to hers.

Her eyes went huge. "Wait—you've never—"

I shook my head.

I had done a lot of stuff, probably more than a lot of guys my age, but I had never gone down on a girl.

Being a shifter, scent was a major thing. Our sense of smell was akin to that of our wolf, heightened and precise. The one time I attempted going down on another girl, I knew immediately she wasn't Larkin. Something about her scent curdled in my stomach, an inherent wrongness I couldn't shake.

I barely managed to stop myself from throwing up on her, feigning a stomach virus and getting out of her room as fast as possible.

I never tried it again.

I looked up at Larkin through my lashes, hoping like hell she didn't notice how unsure I was. "Can I taste you?"

Soundlessly, she nodded.

I slowly peeled her leggings down, exposing inch after inch of creamy flesh. I counted the freckles, traced the scar on her left knee with my tongue. I remembered that scar. She had fallen off her bike and scraped the hell out of her knee.

Remy and I had literally carried her back to her house, leaving our bikes in the alley where she skidded out. It had bled for five blocks.

I tossed the gray pants onto the floor before gently easing her thighs open more. Her hips jerked when I began tracing the edge of the lace panties she wore. I tried to pay attention, taking note when her breathing hitched or her hips moved, but mostly I was absolutely entranced by the girl I was touching.

My index finger ghosted over the wet center of her panties, and she dug her fingers into the couch cushions.

I leaned forward, nuzzling between her legs and inhaling deeply.

Home.

Larkin smelled like home.

I licked her through the lace, smirking when she grabbed a handful of my hair in her hand, rocking her hips.

Slowly, I pulled the lace away from her body, down her legs, until she was fully exposed to me.

Forget alcohol, Larkin made me drunk all on her own.

I slowly nibbled around the exposed flesh, my tongue soothing what my teeth scraped. The taste of her was heady and exotic. The small taste I had when I licked her arousal off my fingers the night before was nothing compared to this. I groaned as I closed my lips over her clit and sucked her into my mouth.

She half-moaned, half-screamed. It was a sound I wanted to hear over and over and over. Fuck, I would record it and make it my ringtone.

It was nothing to slide a finger, then two into her. Her body was wet and soft, ready for my intrusion. I timed the thrust of my fingers with the pull of my mouth until she was gasping, her fingers tugging painfully on my hair.

I worked her over, tasting every inch. I could feel her body shuddering around me, coiling tighter and tighter. I curled my fingers into her, hitting that magic spot that seemed to drive women crazy as I sucked hard.

With a scream of sheer pleasure, Larkin went off. I kept pumping into her, licking her flesh, as I dragged out her orgasm until she was whimpering, her entire body shuddering with aftershocks.

I lifted my head, wiping my mouth on the back of my hand before reaching up and yanking her down off the couch into my arms. Her sensitive core rubbed against my jeans as I hauled her against me, her entire body shaking for a second at the contact.

She dropped her head to my shoulder, her body completely relaxed and spent. She barely had the strength to loop her arms around my neck and her legs around my waist, clinging to me.

My dick throbbed in my jeans, and I was pretty sure I would have a permanent zipper imprint on it moving forward, but I wasn't going to move the girl curled in my arms for the world.

9

LARKIN

My legs were jelly the rest of the day. Rhodes smirked the whole time he helped me get my pants back on, his fingers 'accidentally' brushing places that had my nerve endings waking up all over again.

I had reached for him, wanting to return the favor, but he shot me down with a quick kiss, telling me there was no rush.

Which was good since I was pretty sure my knees wouldn't have supported my weight for what I intended to do.

We hung out in the garage again. Rhodes worked on his motorcycle while I handed him random tools. The only difference now was when he stood up to walk around me, I usually got a kiss out of it.

That, and I finally had my best friend back.

It felt like old times, chatting and joking, an oldies rock station playing from the radio on the workbench.

I watched the muscles in his arm strain as he tightened a bolt. I could watch him do this all freaking day.

"Were you serious about being a janitor?" I asked, finally asking the question that had been bugging me since our chat in the snow days earlier. "I mean, I know you don't want to go to college, but is that what you're going to do the rest of your life?" I tried my best to hide the disappointment in my tone.

Career day had always been fun at school. I loved imagining what I could be in the future, but Rhodes had always taken it as a joke, laughing off the future whenever it was brought up.

One year he said he wanted to raise llamas, the next year he wanted to be a full time lifeguard. Every year it got sillier and more ridiculous, always earning a laugh from kids in our class and even the teachers. But Rhodes never committed to anything.

He pressed his mouth together, grunting as he kept tightening. "Mr. Forbes asked me to come work at the garage. I might apprentice there this summer. He's getting older, so maybe I would run that one day? I don't know. It would be kind of cool to have my own garage."

"That would be awesome," I agreed quickly. I could see him doing that. He had some stupidly natural gift with engines and motors; he understood them. I had seen how excited he got when working on a new project, spending hours online to read up about styles and trim and a whole lot of other stuff I was completely oblivious to. "But you know you could always take classes, too. Get a business degree to go with it?"

He gave me a look. "I know. If I want to, I can go to the community college in Nelson."

I kept smiling. Kept nodding. "Right."

He set the wrench down, giving me his full attention. "Lark, I told you—college and I aren't the best fit."

"Unless you're screwing copious amounts of sorority

girls?" I snarked, remembering what he said the day before.

"I didn't know you were joining a sorority," he replied instantly, flashing me a warm grin.

Damn, he was good.

He stood up, coming over and kissing me again, his mouth firm on mine. "You're the only girl I plan on screwing."

"Good answer," I whispered, trying to control the flock of birds that took flight in my stomach.

Still grinning, he headed to the work bench and pulled out another tool before heading back to the bike.

"But it could be fun," I said slowly. "Remy and Skye, you and me? We could all stay together. Katy said Maren is thinking about coming down here for college, too."

When the Blackwater pack started attending Washington State Eastern University several decades back, they still kept their distance from the normals on campus. The pack had bought a couple of smaller houses on the fringes of the college town for students to use. Over the years they had become unofficial dorms for the pack to use at school.

As if on cue, my phone went off, alerting me to a new text message.

SKYE: *I think I hate snow.*

I laughed down at my phone.

"What?" Rhodes asked.

I waved the phone. "Skye. She hates snow."

LARKIN: *Why?*

SKYE: *I haven't seen Remy in over 24 hours. Also, it's freaking cold. We didn't have snow in the south.*

LARKIN: *You could always shift and go to his house…*

SKYE: *I would, but there's been some power outages and stuff happening. He's been helping his dad and the Council.*

LARKIN: *Ah, yes. The life of the Alpha's mate.*
SKYE: *...so I need to get used to it?*
LARKIN: *Probably*
SKYE: *What about you? I can always shift and come over to hang out.*

I glanced at Rhodes. As much as I wanted to hang out with my best girl, I loved the alone time with my best boy.

SKYE: *U still there?*
LARKIN: *I'm hanging out with Rhodes*
SKYE: *Reeeeeeally? How's that going?*

I bit my lip, wanting to tell her everything and wanting to tell her nothing.

Right now Rhodes and I existed in a perfect bubble.

LARKIN: *Really good.*
SKYE: *Like REALLY good? Or really good?*
LARKIN: *REALLY REALLY*
SKYE: *You better call me with all of the details later!*
LARKIN: *I will. Promise.*

I put my phone back in my pocket.

"How's Skywalker?" he asked, glancing up with a grin.

"Good. Hating the snow. Missing Remy."

He shook his head. "I don't know how they do it."

I leaned forward, head cocked to the side. "Do what?"

"The whole mate bond," he said, exhaling loudly. "I don't know how Remy can handle not being with her all the time. I mean, I hated being away from you when I was taking a shower so—"

"Really?" I asked curiously, my body warming.

His hot gaze landed firmly on me. "Really." Then he gave a small shrug. "It's probably why he asked her to move in with him when we get back to school."

That caught my attention. Skye hadn't mentioned that.

"He did?"

Rhodes nodded. "She isn't sure if she's ready for the move-in stage yet, but the offer is on the table."

"Where would you go?" I asked curiously.

"Hand me a screwdriver?" he asked, reaching a hand out. He waited until I handed it to him before continuing. "I could go to the dorms, but Remy said he wanted me to stay. There's plenty of room. We'll see."

"It would be weird not rooming with her," I murmured, toying with the end of my braid. "I mean, I've only known her a few months, but Skye is ... she's one of my best friends. It's like having a sister."

"You guys wouldn't need to share a room this semester anyway," he reminded me, tossing the screwdriver aside. "There's going to be plenty of rooms."

I scooped it up and put it back in the tool box. "Because of the packs that left?"

He nodded, wiping his dirty hands on a rag. "Gabe said that half the packs have pulled out of the school charter. They're starting their own school, probably in Canada or Michigan. Around the lakes."

"No more Trace," I whispered, relief filling every part of me.

His face tightened with anger, his eyes going flat and hard. "Unfortunately that means I'll have to drive to New York to kick his ass."

"Skye seems like she's doing okay," I said slowly. When I thought of how close she had come to dying, it still made me sick. I hated that I had been sitting in class when she and Rhodes were attacked.

"Skye isn't the only one he hurt," Rhodes said coldly, tossing the rag down with more force than necessary.

"I'm okay, too," I told him gently.

Except for the nightmares.

In my nightmares, Skye didn't interrupt him. In my nightmares, he never stopped.

Shuddering, I stood up and wrapped my arms around myself.

Rhodes swore under his breath, coming over and pulling me into his embrace, his arms banding around me like steel.

"I'm so sorry I wasn't there," he whispered, emotion choking his tone.

My arms went around his waist, taking comfort in the shelter he offered. "It's over. And Trace lost. Now he can't hurt any of us anymore."

"Remy said Skye still has nightmares about what happened to her before," Rhodes said quietly, his lips moving against my hair as he spoke.

I hated the lingering bits of trauma from what Trace had done. Logically I knew I hadn't done anything wrong, but the shame and self-doubt was still there in the dark moments.

But it was harder to feel those moments around Rhodes.

I pulled away from him, and he let me go. His dark eyes watched me walk across the room.

"I have nightmares sometimes, too," I admitted hoarsely. "It helps knowing I won't have to see him again."

He was practically vibrating with rage, but he was swallowing it down for me.

"I'm here for whatever you need, baby," he vowed gently. "If you ever want to talk, or need something, I'm here. I'm sorry I couldn't stop him before."

I walked slowly back to him. "I know. And having you here helps." I sighed as his arms surrounded me again. "I've missed being able to talk to you."

He kissed my forehead, and I tipped my head back, offering my mouth to him.

He didn't hesitate to kiss me fully, his lips hungrily moving over mine until my knees started going back to their gelatinous state.

I knew his hands were smeared with grease and dirt, and probably ruining my clothes, but I didn't really care as his fingers dug into my hips, pulling me as close as our clothes would allow.

The song on the radio changed, something with a deeper bass and heavier tone that had me rolling my hips against his. I gasped when he fisted my braid, yanking my head to the side to attack my neck. His teeth scraped down my skin as he backed me up until my butt hit the workbench ledge.

His hands tightened and he moved to lift me up, but I pulled back, stepping around him so his back was to the work bench.

"Wait," I panted, a hand pressed to his chest.

His eyes glittered, but he did as I asked. His chest heaved as I stepped back and licked my lips.

"Can I …" I exhaled slowly, pulling myself together. "Can I touch you?"

He visibly swallowed, his Adam's apple bobbing as he nodded slowly.

I stepped forward, resting my hand against his stomach. I felt the muscles under my hands spasm. His gaze was hooded as he watched me, quietly letting me slip my hand under his shirt.

He flinched when my hand touched his skin. I could feel the electricity between us pulsing and pulling. A tangible tether connecting us as I slid my hand down, unbuttoning his jeans.

I kept my eyes locked on his the entire time. I saw every emotion there as I pushed the zipper down and slipped my hand under the band of his boxers. My hand brushed the hard length of him, and he hissed through his teeth, his eyes sliding shut.

I pulled my hand back, grinning. "Ah, ah," I chided. "Eyes on me."

His eyes flew open, burning as he stared at me. His hands clenched around the edge of the work bench, and I heard the wood groan and crack under the force of his grip.

I slipped my hand back inside his boxers, slowly tracing the length of him. When I ran a finger along the vein that pulsed on the underside of his erection, his mouth fell open with a ragged breath.

I repeated the action, smiling when his breath caught again.

My fingers swirled around the soft tip of him, feeling the slight moisture there. I collected it on my finger and removed my hands from his pants, licking the salty wetness from the tip of my finger.

A low growl rumbled out of his chest, his eyes dark and starving as he watched me.

More wood splintered under his hold.

I knew he was seconds from grabbing me and hauling me onto the bench. And as much as I wanted his hands, his mouth, between my legs again, I was still curious.

I kept my eyes on his as I slid to my knees in front of him.

"Larkin." He choked on my name as I started tugging his jeans and then boxers down.

His length sprang free, and I tried to hide the shock on my face at the sheer size of him.

His cock was long and thick, weeping at the tip. My

mouth watered for another taste of the salty tang I had on my tongue seconds earlier.

Gripping the base of him, I slowly licked around his cock. I kept my eyes on him, watching to see what he liked.

He really seemed to love when I lifted a hand to test the weight of his balls in my palm. He definitely loved me licking the vein running underneath his cock. But he swore violently when I sucked the tip of him into my mouth, my tongue teasing the slit I discovered.

The iron grip he had on the workbench eased and his hand reached out to touch my head. The touch was gentle at first, but he fisted my braid again when I sucked more of him into my mouth, angling me where he wanted.

"Jesus," he whispered, his head falling back in ecstasy as I eased more of him into my mouth. His hips moved in small, shallow thrusts against my mouth. By the strain in his face, I could tell he was holding himself back as much as he could. Each pass, each bob of my head, I gained ground until I felt him touch the back of my throat.

I swallowed around him, almost jumping when he groaned loudly.

"*Fuck*, Larkin," he hissed, chest heaving. His head fell down, his eyes barely focused. "That ... *Fuck*."

Assuming that was a good thing, I did it again. Then again.

The fourth time, he pulled on my braid hard, trying to pull me off of him.

"Lark, I'm gonna-"

Smirking to myself, I let him slide all the way out until my lips ringed just the tip of him. I sucked hard, quickly pulling the length of him back into my mouth and swallowing around him once more.

With a ragged cry, his hips jerked and I felt him pulsing in my mouth. I kept swallowing his release until he sagged against the bench, the hand gripping my hair relaxing.

I swirled my tongue around him one last time before letting him go and leaning back on my heels to look up at him.

Rhodes was still breathing hard, his chin on his chest, dark hair falling over his face as he caught his breath.

"Was that ... okay?" I asked softly, not sure I had done that exactly right. I had gone with my gut ... and maybe tried to imitate what I had read in a couple romance novels.

His eyes snapped open and he grabbed me, lifting me up and kissing me roughly, desperately.

Now I was the one gasping when he pulled back.

"That was fucking perfect," he whispered, his voice filled with awe. "Do I want to know where you learned to do that?"

Ducking my head into his chest I laughed. "You were definitely the first."

His arms closed around me. "And I better be the only."

"If you insist," I whispered against him.

I pulled away so he could get dressed and started cracking up when I caught a glimpse of his shirt again.

Rhodes paused in the midst of pulling his jeans up, arching a brow as he looked at me. "Baby, laughter isn't something a guy likes to hear when his pants are around his ankles."

I pointed at him. "Rhodes. Your shirt."

The t-shirt he wore that still said "No Pants Are The Best Pants".

He smirked and pulled his jeans on.

I definitely loved that shirt.

10

LARKIN

ALL THE LIGHTS AND TELEVISION WENT DARK WITH A QUIET pop somewhere in the second *Matrix* movie. Rhodes had won the movie choice, but I was counting it a win since I had spent three hours snuggled against his side.

I sat up suddenly, the only light in the room coming from the moonlight glinting off the snow and the fireplace. Rhodes had lit it before we started watching movies. He knew I was a sucker for winter and cozy fireplaces.

"Guess the snow and ice got too heavy for the power lines," Rhodes commented off-handedly.

The stark quiet was deafening between us.

"So, what do we do now?" I asked hesitantly.

He sighed. "I guess we'll never know if they find the Source."

I glanced back over my shoulder. "Like you haven't seen this movie a dozen times."

He shrugged, but grinned at me. "We could play a game."

I perked up, turning to face him on the couch. "Like Clue? Monopoly?" I had a serious love of board games.

He winced and laughed softly. "Baby girl, that's *not* what I had in mind."

Narrowing my eyes, I leaned my shoulder against the back of the couch. "Okay, Mr. I'm-Too-Good-For-Board-Games, what game do you want to play?"

His eyes sparkled sinfully in the low light. "Truth or Dare?"

"I am *not* sitting outside in the snow in my pjs," I quickly protested, shaking my head. At Katy's thirteenth birthday party, she convinced us all to play Truth or Dare. I wound up sitting outside in the dark for twenty minutes, alone, in my pajamas.

Remy and Rhodes had decided to scare the hell out of me. I screamed so loud that it woke up Remy's parents.

Rhodes snorted. "Like I want any part of you getting frostbite." His smile turned predatory. "The only *bite* you get is from me."

I shivered, ducking my head. "Pick a different game."

"Never Have I Ever?" he asked after a second.

"Isn't that a drinking game?" I wasn't crazy about the taste of alcohol, and I knew Rhodes avoided it like the plague. He never would admit it, but I think he was worried he would become as addicted as his father.

"So we play for different stakes," he answered smoothly. Something in his tone had my stomach clenching.

Okay, and other parts clenching.

"Like?"

His hand reached out, his fingers plucking at the hem of my shirt. "Instead of taking a drink, you take off an article of clothing."

My stomach swooped and dipped so fast it made my head spin. My brain was still trying to process his suggestion, but my core throbbed at the idea.

"I'm kidding—"

"Okay," I said softly, cutting him off before he could brush off the suggestion as a joke.

His brows flew up. "Lark, I was teasing."

I leaned forward. "Never have I ever ... had sex."

His jaw dropped open for a second before he snapped it shut, his dark eyes narrowing. "Cheap shot, baby." But he didn't hesitate to pull his shirt over his head and toss it to the floor.

I swallowed hard, trying to look anywhere but the sculpted planes of his chest and torso, the way his muscles rippled and moved with every breath.

"My turn?" he asked, his tone amused. I looked up to see him smirking at me.

"Go for it," I said, squaring my shoulders bravely even as my insides shook.

"Never have I ever shoplifted," he said smugly.

"Rhodes!" I slapped his arm. "One freaking time!"

I had shoplifted. Once.

I had wanted a candy bar when I was six and my mom told me no. I took it anyway, but finally broke down crying in the car before we even left the store parking lot, the chocolate melting in my pocket. I told her I didn't want to go to jail forever.

And Rhodes only knew this because at Katy's birthday party, I had to answer the 'What was the worst thing you ever did?' question during a round of Truth.

"Doesn't make it any less true," he said with a grin.

"Maybe we should play a game that doesn't involve how

well we know each other," I muttered, pulling off my shirt. I wished I had put on a camisole or something, but all I had now was my bra as my shirt joined his in the discard pile.

At least it was the black lace bra and matching panty set that Katy had convinced me to get a few months back. She argued girls needed to feel sexy for themselves.

Judging by the way Rhodes' throat was working, I owed her a thank you.

He cleared his throat, his voice rougher. "Your turn."

I sucked in a deep breath, thinking, but fully aware of the way his gaze tracked the heavy rise and fall of my chest. My nipples tightened, and it wasn't entirely from the chill in the air.

"Never have I ever lived with an alpha," I said.

He rolled his eyes, but pulled off a sock.

"Never have I ever gone vegan."

Now I rolled my eyes. A few years back I had the brilliant thought to go vegan because I read *The Jungle* for an extra credit project. I definitely didn't factor in my wolf's need for meat in my diet. It had lasted all of fifteen hours until the next morning when I had eaten almost an entire pound of bacon for breakfast.

I yanked off one of my socks, making a show of dropping it.

"Never have I ever jumped off a roof." I made a face at him as I said it, remembering when he and Ryder dared each other to jump off the roof over the front porch of the Brooks Ridge cabin at school.

Ryder had broken his wrist, and Rhodes had severely sprained an ankle. It scared the hell out me seeing him slam into the ground.

Off went his second sock.

"You have more clothes on than I do," he said, touching the strap of my bra.

I arched a brow. "You picked this game, remember?"

"Never have I ever broken curfew."

"You've never *had* a curfew!" I sputtered. Rhodes's dad had barely been coherent most days. He could hardly manage himself, let alone parent Rhodes.

"And?"

With a huff I jerked off my last sock.

"Happy?"

"Elated," he deadpanned dryly. "I've always had a huge thing for your toes."

Lifting a foot, I jabbed him with my toes playfully. He caught my foot, tickling the arch. With a shriek, I pulled away laughing. I tucked my foot under my body to protect it.

"Jerk." I stuck my tongue out at him.

I barely managed to get my tongue past my lips before his mouth was on mine, his tongue sweeping into my mouth and his breath mingling with mine.

Rhodes pulled back, his nose barely brushing mine. "Next time you want me to kiss you, just ask. You don't have to flash your tongue at me."

I wanted to laugh, but a steady pulse started pounding between my thighs as soon as his mouth touched mine.

I was seriously in trouble.

Clearing my throat, I smiled at him. "My turn," I whispered.

He stayed close to me, his eyes studying my face.

"Never have I ever …" I paused, gathering myself and trying hard not to blush. "Gone down on a girl."

His eyes flared wide, something dark and hungry swirling there. He never broke eye contact as he reached down and undid the button on his jeans, lifting his hips and tugging them down. He kicked them off impatiently.

I bit my lip, my eyes catching the impressive length tenting his boxers. My mouth watered, remembering the taste and feel of him in my mouth.

"Never have I ever," he said softly, reaching over to trace my jaw, "given a blow job."

His thumb traced the seam of my mouth, and I sucked it in, my teeth sinking into his flesh as I swirled my tongue around the pad of his thumb. His breath caught, eyes drooping as he watched me.

I let him go and stood up, pulling my leggings down and stepping out of them. Instead of going back to my seat on the couch, I moved between his spread legs, looking down at him. His hands slowly teased the skin of my thighs, deliberately skirting away from any area covered by my panties.

"Never have I ever touched myself thinking about someone in this room," I said, my voice barely a breath as I watched his expression turn ravenous.

Reaching back, I undid the clasp of the bra, letting it fall to the ground in a whisper of fabric. Rhodes groaned, the low sound making me slick and wet.

Exhaling a ragged breath, Rhodes reached down and slipped out of his boxers. I helped pull them the rest of the way off when he got to his knees. His cock sprung curved up, hard and ready, resting against his abdomen.

I slowly straddled his thighs, easing my weight onto him.

His fingers grazed the center of my panties, my hips jerking.

"You win," he murmured. His eyes lifted to mine. "Name your prize."

I looped my arms around his neck, pulling his face to mine.

"You," I replied. "I want *you*."

He wrapped his arms around me, pulling me flush against his chest and kissing me hard. His mouth slanted over mine, demanding and hot and wet. I opened to him, yielding with a low moan.

He kept one arm banded around me, but the other slid up my side and around the front, slowly teasing my breast, tugging at the hard peak.

With a gasp, I jerked my mouth away, my head falling back as he rolled my nipple between his skilled fingers. His lips attacked my neck, moving across the column of my throat. His hips lifted, thrusting up into me, his length hitting my clit just right.

I cried out, my hands fisting in his hair and I tried not to topple over from the sensation.

After a few minutes of grinding against him as he plucked at my nipples, teasing and tormenting them with equal attention, I grabbed his shoulders.

"More," I begged, rolling my hips again.

His hands moved to my panties, shoving them aside and sinking a finger into me, his thumb stroking the side of my clit.

"*More*," I demanded, riding his hand.

He added a second finger, watching with rapt attention as his fingers disappeared into my body.

I scraped my nails across the back of his neck, twisting my hands into his hair and jerking his head up.

I almost came from the expression in his dark eyes alone when they bore into mine.

"More," I whispered. "I want all of you."

Understanding dawned in his eyes, the steady slide of his fingers through my wet flesh become less rhythmic. His chest heaved.

"Larkin." He swallowed.

I reached down, circling him with my hand and dragging the tip of his against me.

I gasped the second his hot skin touched mine, branding me. My head fell forward onto his shoulder.

"Rhodes, *please*," I whimpered.

"Larkin, look at me," he said softly.

I lifted my head, stunned to see the hesitance warring with want in his face. His jaw was tight, his body trembled under mine as he tried to restrain himself.

"I've never ..."

I slowed my hips. "You've never what?"

He glanced down at where I had been sliding against him. "I've always used a condom. I've never-"

Wait, was Rhodes actually blushing?

That made no sense. One of the best parts of being a shifter, or so I was told, was that we were immune to most STIs that normals dealt with. An added benefit of our mixed DNA or healing. Since females didn't become fertile until they were at least in their early twenties, pregnancy wasn't an issue either.

From what I understood and heard, condoms weren't a thing most shifters used.

"You used condoms?" I tried to figure out why he was telling me this now.

He nodded slowly, his gaze unreadable as he watched me.

"Okay," I said softly. "Go get one."

"No," he said, frowning. "I always used one because ... it didn't feel right. The same way I couldn't go down on another girl, the idea of marking her didn't seem right either."

He lifted the hand not currently still inside my body to my face.

"Until you. It's always been you." His whispered words cracked open something in my heart. "I don't want to use one with you."

"Then don't," I told him, leaning forward to kiss him slowly, deeply. "Just be with me."

His mouth moved against mine, gentle at first, then growing hungrier. His fingers found the maddening rhythm from before until I broke our kiss with a cry.

"Rhodes."

He stood up in one fluid motion, lifting me in one arm and moving us to the floor. He laid me down in front of the fireplace, kneeling between my spread legs.

With agonizingly slow movements, he peeled my panties down my legs, his gaze turning molten as he stared at me, completely bare and exposed.

"You're fucking stunning," he told me, smoothing his hands across my hips.

Instead of the uncertainty and shyness I had expected, I relaxed against the carpet, letting him look all he wanted. There was no room for embarrassment with the way he was gazing down at me, a mix of lust and love in his eyes.

"Are you sure?" he asked quietly.

I lifted a brow, a smile tugging at my lips. "I'm sure that if you don't do something soon, I'll finish this without you."

A low growl rumbled out of his throat. "Not fucking happening, baby."

He lowered himself onto me, kissing his way from my collarbone to the place where my hip met my thigh.

Spreading my legs open more, he swiped the flat of his tongue across me, my back arching off the floor.

Using his thumbs, he spread me open further, feasting on me until I was writhing and crying out, just this side of exploding.

When I was about to scream, he lifted up, reaching down to position himself at my opening. He flexed his hips towards me, a shallow thrust that made me gasp.

He was barely inside, but I already knew he was bigger than the two fingers he had slid into me earlier.

"Breathe, Lark," he encouraged me softly, making sure to watch my face the whole time.

I sucked in a deep breath, tentatively lifting my hips to take more of him into me. The pressure was like nothing I had ever felt, my body stretching around him. It wasn't painful, but it wasn't the most pleasant experience either.

"Hey," he said quietly, waiting for me to meet his gaze. "Are you sure?"

I reached up, framing his face with my hands. "I've been in love with you since I was thirteen," I whispered, watching his eyes go wide and wondrous. "It's always been *you*."

With a single thrust, he seated himself fully into me. I cried out at the sudden, sharp pain, tears pricking my eyes.

Wow, that hurt more than I expected.

I focused on breathing, adjusting to the feeling of him inside of me.

"I'm sorry, baby," he whispered, his tone absolutely gutted. His arms shook as he forced himself to stay perfectly still above me, inside me.

"It's okay," I gasped, the pain starting to ebb. All I was left with was a heavy fullness that made me dizzy.

After a few long seconds, Rhodes slowly pulled almost

completely out of me and then slid back inside. My body still flinched at the intrusion, but each thrust was easier, better, than the next. By the fourth time he slid back into me, I was lifting my hips to meet him thrust for thrust.

"Faster," I urged, needing him to pick up the pace. The orgasm he had nearly wrung from me earlier was roaring back to the surface, but I needed *more*.

"Hold onto me," he choked out, his hips snapping faster against me, grinding down harder with each pass.

I wrapped my arms around him, sucking in a breath through my teeth as my body tensed, chasing that high I knew was *right there*.

He lifted my hips, angling me so his thrusts went deeper, hitting a spot inside of me that made me cry out in sheer pleasure, the feeling so intense it bordered on too much.

He slicked his finger in firm circles around my clit, teasing and pressing until I tumbled into oblivion. My body shattered, convulsing and clenching around him, my nails scoring his back viciously as I tried to find anything to tether me to this world.

With a roar, Rhodes followed me over the edge, jerking into me several times.

He all but collapsed on me, his body heaving on top of mine as we both came back down, came back to earth.

I stroked his hair softly, my heart thumping in my chest, blood pumping in my ears.

He lifted his head, his brown eyes soft and full of love. He kissed me slowly, gently, as we both came down from the high.

"I love you, too, baby girl," he whispered against my mouth.

11

RHODES

I WAS COMPLETELY FUCKED. THERE WAS ABSOLUTELY NO WAY I was ever going to recover from the last twelve hours.

I moved inside of Larkin, her cries getting louder the harder I drove into her. Her dark hair was splayed across my pillows, fanned out around her head like a mahogany curtain of silk. Her dark eyes were screwed shut as I lightly pinched her clit, pulling her over the edge of her climax.

Her impossibly tight pussy spasmed around me, dragging me into yet another release that left me lightheaded and seeing spots. I rolled off her when we finished, thankful we had finally made it up to my bed.

Waking up with Larkin after last night had been incredible.

Waking up to her hand stroking my dick was even better.

I hadn't planned on taking her again since I knew she had to be sore, but my girl definitely wasn't taking 'no' for an answer.

And I definitely didn't say no when she took me in her hand, guiding me into her body. Not when I looked down, seeing the way the early morning light broke across her naked skin, the rosy flush of her chest and cheeks as she gasped, her arousal climbing higher.

I reached out, tugging her into my side. In true Larkin fashion, she cuddled into my side like a kitten, sated and sleepy. My lips kissed her hairline and I took a deep breath, my wolf practically vibrating with pleasure at the scent of me on Larkin. Our essences mingled together, an intoxicating blend that had my dick ready for another round.

"Why don't I make breakfast?" I suggested softly, glancing down at her.

She tipped her head up, her tiny nose wrinkling. "You're going to cook?"

Okay, so cooking wasn't exactly my forte. I was more a microwave and toaster kind of guy.

I rolled my eyes. "I think I can figure out a way to feed you."

Her stomach growled loudly and she grinned sheepishly at me. "Food sounds good. Is it okay if I jump in the shower?"

Some deep part of me hated the idea of her washing my scent off of her, but I wasn't going to tell her that. My wolf was a possessive asshole who wanted everyone, especially a pair of annoying as fuck twins, to know Larkin was ours.

"Of course," I replied. I got up and went to my dresser, pulling on my clothes as I looked out the window. "Looks like the snow plows came through last night," I told her, seeing patches of black on the road.

I felt Larkin press herself against my back, looking over my shoulder. Her very naked breasts were flush against my spine, and I groaned quietly.

"I thought you wanted food," I said lightly.

"Maybe I had a different kind of food in mind?" she said innocently, her hands delving under my shirt, her nails raking down my abs.

"God, you're fucking insatiable," I muttered, turning in her arms and kissing her soundly, my hands cupping her cheeks. I pulled back, holding her.

"Food first so you have the energy for me to fuck you later," I told her.

Her eyes lit up. "I like that plan."

Shaking my head, I walked out of my room and headed downstairs to make breakfast. As soon as I got into the kitchen, I realized the power was still out which left us with the option of cereal or cereal.

I pulled out the three kinds we had and a couple of bowls for her to make her choice when she came downstairs. Maybe the power was on in town and we could get to the café since the roads were cleared. I could text Skye and see if she knew. Her mom basically ran the place now.

I found my phone in the living room but the battery was dead. I tossed it back onto the couch as someone knocked on the front door.

I glanced around the room, quickly gathering all of our discarded clothes from last night into a pile and tossing them to the side of the couch, not that it would do much to mask the scent of what happened here hours earlier.

I could still smell both of us in the room, and if someone wasn't knocking on the door again, I would've headed upstairs to join her in the shower.

I made my way to the front door and pulled it open, stunned to see Gabe and Remy on the other side.

"Checking to make sure everyone survived the power outage?" I joked with a grin, leaning against the door frame.

Remy gave me a tight smile. "Hey, man. Can we come in?"

I knew my best friend enough to know something was wrong. Not just power outages in the pack wrong, but something worse.

I straightened, looking from Remy to Gabe. The Alpha looked serious and somber. I stepped back, letting them into the foyer.

"What's going on?" I asked, the question barely out of my mouth before I heard footsteps on the stairs. Seconds later, Larkin came around the corner.

"Hey, Rhodes, do you have—" She stopped short abruptly, her eyes going huge as she looked at Gabe and Remy. At least she had taken the time to slip one of my shirts on before coming downstairs.

If she would have come down naked…

My wolf growled in my chest at the thought. I really didn't want to have to tear out the eyes of my best friend and my Alpha for seeing her naked.

"Um, hi," she squeaked, her big eyes going to me.

"Hey, Lark," Remy said, his tone giving off a lot of confusion as he glanced from her to me.

"Larkin, how are you?" Gabe asked politely, not looking the least bit unsure of the situation.

"I'm good, Sir," she answered, taking a step backwards. "I should just … go? Yeah. I'm gonna go."

She didn't wait for any of us to reply before spinning and thundering back up the stairs. A second later I heard my bedroom door slam shut.

I shoved my hands into the pockets of my jeans as Remy gave me an incredulous look.

"What's going on?" I repeated, trying to get back on track so I could go upstairs and join my—

I froze, realizing I was about to say *girlfriend*.

Gabe cleared his throat. "Rhodes, it's about your father."

Fucking hell.

My stupid heart sank as hope I hadn't even realized I was holding onto popped like a useless balloon.

I masked any emotion on my face and sighed. "Couldn't stay sober even in rehab, huh?" I snorted, shaking my head. "I don't know why I thought this time would be any different."

Remy shifted on his feet. "Rhodes—"

I held up a hand. "Don't, man. It's fine. It's par for the fucking course."

"Son, you don't understand," Gabe said slowly.

"That my dad is a drunk?" I scoffed. "Trust me, *that* I absolutely understand. So, what happens now? Are they kicking him out? Or is he going to try one more time to be an actual father?"

"Rhodes, stop," Remy said, his tone bordering on desperate. "Just stop. You need to listen."

I grit my teeth. "If this is the part where you tell me to give him one more chance, I swear to Christ, Rem—"

"Rhodes, your father is dead."

Everything stopped.

I even held my breath as I slowly turned to look at Gabe.

With a long sigh, Gabe stepped forward, his hand reaching out to land on my shoulder. It was a gesture of comfort, something a father would do.

Something *my* father would never do.

"The center called me this morning," he started. "They went in to check on your father and found his body."

Found his body.

"How?" I managed to get out. "How did he die?"

Gabe's eyes slid shut, shaking his head once. "That doesn't matter now."

"The hell it doesn't," I snarled, jerking away. "What happened?"

Remy exchanged a look with his father before looking at me.

"He killed himself early this morning," Remy finally said quietly.

I staggered back a step, the news a physical blow. "He *what?* How?"

Gabe was already shaking his head. "Son—"

"Don't tell me it doesn't matter," I snapped viciously, lashing out. "How did he do it?"

Gabe never stopped watching me. "He broke the mirror in his bathroom. He used the glass to …"

I nodded, getting the picture, vividly, in my head. Drawing in a slow breath, I rubbed a hand along my jaw.

"Okay." That simple little word was all I could manage.

Gabe kept his steady gaze locked on me. "We've already arranged transport for him to be returned to Blackwater. We can discuss funeral arrangements, or Mallory has offered to handle them all if you like."

"That's fine," I agreed. I didn't have the first clue about planning a funeral. Weren't funerals expensive?

"Why don't you pack a bag and come stay with us for the rest of the break?" Gabe suggested gently. "We'll make a plan, figure out what to do next."

"No, thanks." The last thing I wanted was to be surrounded by the ever-amazing Holts in all their nuclear family perfection. I didn't need the pity or the sympathy.

"Rhodes, seriously," Remy said, touching my arm. "Just come stay with us for a few days."

"I'm good," I told him, my mouth speaking without prompting. My brain was still buzzing, a void of white noise eating away at me.

"Rhodes—"

"I said I'm good," I snapped, tossing a glare at him.

"Fine," Remy said evenly, not at all offended by my tone. He simply took it in stride. "But I'm staying here today."

I opened my mouth, but he shut me up.

"I'm not leaving. I'll sit in the living room and read and you can work in the garage or whatever. We can watch a movie and not talk. But I'm *not* leaving you. You're my best friend, Rhodes. Deal with it." He folded his massive arms across his equally massive chest, staring me down.

With a sigh, I gave a quick nod.

Gabe opened the door. "If you change your mind, the door is always open for you, Rhodes. And I am sorry. I honestly never thought this would happen. It never even crossed my mind. When I spoke to him last week, he seemed good. Upbeat, even."

I flinched. I hadn't tried talking to him once. In the days since he left, I had racked up three missed calls from a number I was pretty sure was his, and just as many unopened voicemails.

What if I had simply answered one fucking call? Would that have been the difference? Was this my fault?

Pain ripped through my chest, almost knocking me over. Guilt swamped me, punching me in the stomach.

As quick as the wave rose up, I slammed it back, putting my emotions on lock down.

Likely seeing the sudden torrent of emotions that tore

through me, Gabe stepped forward. I immediately took a step back, my hands curling into fists.

"The power should be back on within the hour," Gabe informed me, ignoring my blatant refusal at comfort. "You boys call me if you need anything at all."

"Thanks, Dad," Remy spoke up when I stayed silent. All I could do was nod in agreement.

Gabe stepped through the door, sighing as he looked at me. "I'm so sorry, Rhodes."

"Thanks," I muttered, waiting until he turned to head down the stairs before closing the door on his retreating back.

I leaned my head against the cool wood, not wanting to turn around and see my best friend watching me.

Soft footsteps on the stairs were what finally made me turn.

Larkin was standing in the hallway, now wearing my shirt *and* a pair of my gym shorts that looked ready to fall off her tiny hips.

"Hey, Larkin," Remy said softly.

Larkin barely looked at him, her doe brown eyes watching me with worry.

"What happened?" She visibly swallowed. She took a step forward and paused.

I leaned my back against the door. "Apparently Dad had enough of rehab," I said darkly, already feeling the churn of anger in my gut. My shock was slowly wearing off, and now I was getting pissed.

Remy sighed. "Rhodes."

"He left?" Larkin frowned.

"Permanently," I replied with a grimace. I shrugged indifferently. "Apparently he killed himself."

With a shocked gasp, her hands flew to her mouth. She

shook her head in disbelief, her gaze swinging from me to Remy and back to me. A second later she flew across the hallway, launching herself into my arms.

I caught her on reflex, my arms going around her small frame to hold her.

Without thinking, I buried my face in her neck, letting the comfort she offered cover me like a warm blanket. I tightened my hold, squeezing her hard enough that it probably hurt, but she didn't say a single word or try to break free.

Instead she hugged me back just as fiercely.

"I'm right here," she whispered against me, her voice breaking through the incessant buzzing in my head.

And for that moment, I let myself be weak and greedily take all she had to offer.

12

LARKIN

We were ninety minutes in, and I still had no idea what movie we were supposed to be watching.

The power had come back on less than an hour after Gabe left, which was about the time Skye showed up. She gave Rhodes a hug and told him to shut up when he said she didn't need to stay.

We had all made our way into the living room where I quickly scrambled to clean up my clothes, avoiding eye contact with Remy and Skye. I ran back to my own house to take my shower before coming back to Rhodes'.

Everyone was already camped out in the living room with the tv on. I hesitated a second in the doorway, reading the room.

Remy and Skye were curled up together on the loveseat, Skye reading from the ereader Remy had gotten her for Christmas while Rhodes and Remy watched the end of a show.

For a second I wondered if I should sit next to Rhodes or give him space, but the second he looked up, the tight lines around his eyes easing when he saw me, the choice was made. I went to him, sitting down as close as I could and snuggling into his side.

No one spoke as the next movie had started, and I couldn't pay attention.

I wanted to look at Rhodes, to stare at him and study him until I knew what was happening in his head. Despite his arm wrapped around me, I hadn't felt this far away from him in days.

God, I wanted to go back to this morning before Gabe and Remy had shown up. When it was just us in bed.

My stomach swooped at the memories of us together. In bed.

In this very room.

Blinking back the sudden rush of tears I felt, I glanced around the room. My gaze caught on Skye, who looked completely perplexed as she looked at her screen.

"You okay?" I asked, my voice making everyone look at Skye.

Her frown deepened. "What's a *plenipotentiary instrument*?"

Remy choked on the water he had started drinking. He quickly set the glass down on the end table beside the loveseat, twisting to look down at her. "*What?*"

Skye pointed at the screen, her nose still wrinkled in confusion. "It says—"

"What are you reading?" he asked with a laugh, still coughing.

"*The Duke and His Sword*," she answered, looking up.

I couldn't help but start laughing. "Why are you reading that?"

"Because it had good reviews? And it was one of those unlimited books I got," she said defensively. Mallory and

Gabe had gotten her an annual unlimited reader membership to go with the ereader Remy bought.

"So, what is it?" she asked again, looking at Remy and then me.

Even Rhodes seemed to have turned his attention to us for a moment.

I exchanged a look with Remy.

"Um—"

"Whatever, I'll look it up," she muttered, pulling her cell phone out and typing in the phrase. She was quiet for a second while she read.

Then her jaw dropped open, her cheeks heating. "Oh."

Remy's shoulders shook as his arm tightened around her. He bit his lower lip and looked away, eyes laughing.

Skye sighed, flipping the cover shut on the device. "I guess I should have realized this was a sex book when he started calling his sword his 'torrid extension'."

I laughed behind my hand, darting a glance at Rhodes to see a thin smile tugging at his lips.

"Maybe you skip that one, babe?" Remy suggested, kissing the top of her head.

"It had good reviews," she muttered, but turned off the screen with a small grin. "But I *was* getting sick of Lady Tarabella and her constantly sweating petals. That couldn't have been healthy."

I giggled harder, ducking my head into Rhodes's side, relieved when I felt his laughter, too.

For one perfect second, everything felt normal again.

Then Rhodes's phone rang.

He sobered instantly, all traces of happiness gone and that void was back between us. I shivered as he stood up, pulling his phone from the charger and answering it. He stepped into the next room, effectively cutting us all off.

I leaned back against the couch, pulling my knees up to my chest and wrapping my arms around them with a deep sigh.

Skye got up from the love seat and came over, sinking down next to me and hugging me to her side.

"How are you doing?" she asked softly.

I heard Remy get up and head into the kitchen, trying to discreetly give us space.

I sniffled, the wave of tears threatening again. "I don't know what to do. Last night was so … perfect. And now everything's a mess."

Skye bit her lower lip. "So, you two are together now?"

I slowly nodded. "Yeah. I think so."

"You *think* so?"

"The last couple of days have been amazing," I told her honestly. "We both talked about us and decided we want to be together. And last night we …" I blushed, trailing off.

Skye nodded slowly. "Gotcha." She gave me a small smile. "I'm happy for you."

"Everything feels so up in the air now, you know? Like the bubble around us burst and I'm not sure where we stand. I want to talk to him, but that sounds pretty selfish, you know? Trying to figure out where I stand while he's dealing with this."

"What do you want?" she asked me softly.

I leaned my head against her shoulder. "All I want is Rhodes. And I want him to know I'm here for whatever he needs."

"For what it's worth," she said after a beat of silence, "he seems better when you're around. The second you walked back in the door, he relaxed just a little bit. I can't imagine what he's going through, but you need to be there. Let him know you're there, but also be willing to give him some space."

She shrugged lightly, looking back towards the kitchen where Remy was now on his phone.

"That's how Remy got through to me," she added, a smile drifting across her face as she watched him pace to the window, quietly talking to whoever had called. "He didn't push, but I always knew he was there. I was so used to being on my own and not depending on anyone, that I wasn't sure I could. I mean, I had my mom growing up, but you know how bad it was. It took me a while to really let Remy in."

"Rhodes never had any family to rely on," I murmured.

"Not true," she argued. "He's always had you and Remy and Katy. Gabe and Mallory, and your parents. But right now his world just got rocked. He might need to be reminded of all the people who love him. When things go sideways, it's hard not to fall back into survival mode and push everyone away."

"I just want to go back to yesterday," I whispered, sadness lacing my words.

"I know." She leaned her head against mine. "When do your parents come home?"

"Tomorrow," I answered. Part of me was glad—I loved my parents and had a great relationship with them. But I also knew it would be hard spending time with them without Rhodes seeing something he never had.

And now never would.

"And your birthday is Monday," she said, trying to cheer me up.

I wasn't exactly looking forward to my birthday. I knew

there would be a party—there always was. My parents loved making a big deal out of my birthday and the fact that it was New Year's Day. They threw a big New Year's Eve party that doubled as my birthday party every year.

The last thing I could think about right now was a party.

Remy came back into the room, and we glanced up at him.

"Katy's coming home," he told us, sitting back down.

I wasn't surprised. As much as Katy and Rhodes gave each other a hard time, they were basically siblings.

Skye nodded next to me. "She told me earlier she was going to try and get home for the … funeral," she finished softly.

"There isn't going to be one."

All our heads snapped around to see Rhodes in the doorway, his phone clutched tight in his fist.

"What?" I asked, finding my voice first.

Rhodes looked away. "The ground is too hard for a burial. Besides, dad would've hated it. He would rather have his ashes spread on the mountain, so that's what I'll do this spring."

"Are you sure?" Remy asked slowly. "We can still have a memorial."

Rhodes snorted, his expression grim. "What for? My dad had barely been a functioning pack member the last decade."

"For you," I told him. "The memorial would be for you. To get closure."

Shrugging, he pushed his phone into his pocket. "Consider me closed."

Remy exhaled hard. "Rhodes—"

"What do you want me to say, Remy?" he snapped suddenly. "You want me to stand up in front of a room full of people and tell them what a good guy my dad was? About all the memories I have of him teaching me to ride a bike or go camping? I can't do that because that's all shit *your* dad did. My dad sat in that chair," he wildly gestured to the recliner no one had touched, "and drank his life away."

Remy leaned forward, resting his forearms on his legs. "I get that."

"Do you?" he challenged, eyes flashing with so much bitterness and anger that made my heart ache.

"Because you don't know what it's like to come home and make yourself dinner every day. To see all of your friends have these amazing parents and families. I had *me*, Rem. So I'm dealing with this the way that's best for *me*."

"You have us," I said softly. "You have me."

A shadow crossed his face. "Really, Lark? You still want to stick around after this?"

I froze, my heart stopping. "What do you mean?"

"I'm the kid of a deserter and a drunk," he spat. "Is that really something you want?"

I got to my feet suddenly, ready to shake him. "I want *you*, Rhodes."

"I'm a mess," he said softly, shaking his head. His voice broke on the last word.

"Then you're my mess," I replied, walking over to him. "I'm right here. I'm not going anywhere. You aren't alone, Rhodes."

I barely rested my hand against his chest before he was hauling me into his arms, his mouth coming down intense and demanding as he kissed me until I was dizzy.

He pulled back, resting his forehead to mine. "Thanks, baby girl."

"Anytime," I returned just as quietly, fisting my hands in the fabric of his shirt.

He kissed my forehead. "I'm going to go to the garage. Work on the bike."

"You want company?" I offered, wanting to stay with him.

He slowly shook his head. "I think I need to be by myself for a little while. It'll help to focus on the engine for an hour or two."

"Okay," I said, trying to smile. "I can make us all something to eat?"

I could see he wasn't hungry, but he gave me a nod anyway.

"Thanks, Lark."

I shrugged. "No big deal."

"I mean … for being here," he said in a single breath. "For staying."

I wrapped my arms around his narrow waist, hugging him tight. It took everything in me to let him go. To watch as he headed, alone, to the garage. I didn't move until I heard the door shut.

"Finally," Skye muttered behind me.

I spun around.

She smiled at me, her green eyes sparkling. "It's about time you two got your shit together."

Remy smirked, nodding in agreement. "I'm glad you're here for him, Lark. He needs you."

"He needs all of us," I corrected.

"But he needs you most," Skye said as I walked by.

I sighed, brushing my hair away from my face as I walked into the kitchen.

I needed him most, too.

13

RHODES

My hands ached from holding the wrench too tight for the last three hours. I hadn't stopped working on the bike, methodically removing and rebuilding entire sections that honestly didn't need it. I just needed the familiar feel, the control it offered me.

At least I could fix some of the things I broke.

At some point Larkin had dropped off a sandwich on the workbench that went untouched, but I appreciated the gesture and the way she sat silently watching me work for a few minutes before leaving.

About an hour ago Remy had come into the garage. He didn't say anything, just grabbed a set of tools and started working on the back brakes like we had done a dozen times.

Skye had brought us both bottles of water, only pausing to touch my shoulder and then Remy's before leaving.

I appreciated it, the fact that my friends were staying close but still giving me space.

The white noise in my head was still buzzing, blocking

most of what I was thinking and feeling. I needed that mental block right now. I wasn't ready to start figuring things out.

Today I would be numb. Tomorrow I would start to figure shit out.

Like the house.

Jesus, did we have a mortgage? Bills that needed to be paid?

Sighing, I set down the wrench.

Remy didn't lift his head from what he was doing. Instead, he only asked, "What's up?"

"I'm just realizing I have no idea what to do next," I admitted, sitting down on the hard cement of the floor. Within seconds the cold started seeping in.

Remy glanced over. "I would suggest reattaching the engine if you want this thing to actually run."

"I'm talking about my dad," I said quietly.

Remy paused, turning to give me his full attention. "Okay. Let's figure it out."

"Your dad said he ... his body would be back in Blackwater later today." I swallowed around the sudden lump of emotion clogging my throat. "Do I want to see him? Do I *have* to see him? Before they ... cremate him, I mean?"

"I think that's your call, man," he said slowly, his intense eyes studying me, watching me.

"But what do I *do*?" I needed a fucking rule book or manual or some shit on dealing with sudden death of a parent you weren't sure you cared about.

"Rhodes, there's no wrong answer. You do what you think is right," Remy told me firmly. "If that's seeing your dad tonight before he's cremated, then do that. If that's *not* seeing him, that's okay, too."

"What if I don't, and I change my mind later?" I asked, still unsure.

Remy frowned. "Honestly, Rhodes, I don't know what to tell you. That could happen, but if it does, it won't mean you didn't love him any less."

Something in me bristled. "I didn't love him. He was a drunk who couldn't be bothered to be a parent."

Remy dropped his eyes. "Rhodes, you don't mean that."

"Yeah, I do."

"No, you don't," he replied, looking me in the eye. "If you did, you wouldn't be having these thoughts. It wouldn't matter."

I closed my eyes, willing the sudden surge of emotions back.

I didn't want to care. I had spent my whole life *not* caring. It was pointless to give a shit now about a man who couldn't handle a week of sobriety for his son.

"There's nothing wrong with loving your dad," Remy said quietly. "It doesn't make you a weaker man to care about someone else, Rhodes. That's who you are—it's one of the reasons you're my best friend. My beta. I need a guy who can give a shit even when the other person isn't worth it."

I pressed my fist to my forehead. "I shouldn't care."

"Yes, you should," he retorted, heat in his voice. "Your dad not being able to get his life together is on *him*, Rhodes. Your mom being weak enough to walk away from her kid is on *her*. The fact that you haven't let them shut you down means you're stronger than they are."

"The fact that it took me years to admit how I feel about Larkin might prove you wrong," I muttered.

"Bullshit. Larkin is here *with you*." His eyes flashed as he shook his head. "I know you thought you would be too much like your dad or your mom to really commit to any kind of relationship, but it's pretty freaking obvious to anyone that what you and Larkin have is a hell of a lot more than what your parents had."

The garage door opened and Skye poked her head in, her green eyes huge on her face. Huge, and fierce.

Remy was immediately on his feet, with me close behind.

"Someone's at the door," she said in a low tone.

Remy frowned. "Who? Katy's plane doesn't land for another few hours."

I looked at him, stunned. "Katy's coming home? Why?"

"For you, dumbass," he replied, side-eying me. "You have a family that loves you, man. You aren't going through this alone."

"Speaking of family," Skye said quietly, opening the door so we could come into the house. She blocked the doorway leading to the foyer before we could turn the corner.

"Look, say the word and she's gone, okay?" Skye said, the heat in her voice surprising me. "I mean, Larkin's ready to kick her ass already, and I'm happy to help."

"Who's here?" Remy demanded, eyes narrowing.

I could hear voices coming down the hallway. Larkin's and … another.

One I only heard in my dreams.

"My mother," I said slowly.

☪

Larkin

Maggie Rhodes-DeWitt was really freaking pretty. Stupidly pretty, to be honest. It was really easy to see where Rhodes got his looks from. The dark intensity of his eyes, the shade of his dark brown hair, even that tight smile that boarded on a grimace he did whenever he was stressed and tense.

Maggie was flashing me that tight lipped smile now, shifting her weight on her feet nervously.

My wolf growled in me, pacing like a caged animal.

We both wanted to rip her apart.

She was barely inside the door and looked ready to bolt any second, her eyes skittishly moving over every surface and looking anywhere but at me.

Probably because I knew I was glaring at her.

Her expression got even more tense as I heard footsteps coming down the hall. Rhodes came in first, Remy and Skye close behind.

"Rhodes," she breathed, taking a step towards him.

Rhodes countered her by taking a step of his own.

Towards me.

I reached out, grabbing his hand in mine, pressing my side against his arm in support.

Maggie flinched, her eyes dropping. "I guess I deserve that."

"What the hell are you doing here?" he demanded.

She cleared her throat, her eyes skittering around like a deer who stumbled into a pack of wolves. "I ... Can we talk? Please?"

His fingers tightened around mine so hard I almost winced.

But I wasn't letting go for the world.

"What could you possibly have to say?" he asked incredulously. "My dad dies and you decide to stop by for a visit?"

She clasped her hands in front of her, twisting her fingers together anxiously. "I know. I know my timing is awful and you … I know that you just lost your father. But that's why I had to come."

"A little late to put in for that Mother of the Year award," he snarked viciously, his entire body coiled for fight or flight. "You missed the cut off by a solid decade."

She flinched back, nodding in jerky movements. Her chin trembled. "I know, honey. I know. Please, just give me a few minutes. I just … I'll leave as soon as I'm done. I swear."

"Fine," he ground out. "Talk."

"Maybe we could talk … alone?" Maggie nearly whispered the last word.

Rhodes glanced at Remy. They exchanged long looks, but Remy finally nodded. He pulled Skye towards the stairs with him. I started to go with them, but Rhodes's grip on me turned ironclad.

"Larkin stays," he announced firmly.

My heart slammed painfully against my ribs as I brushed my nose against his shoulder for a second.

"We can go sit in the living room," he muttered, heading down the hallway with me. He didn't wait to see if Maggie followed.

Rhodes sat on the couch, pulling me down flush beside him. He let go of my hand only so he could wrap a strong arm around me, anchoring me to his side.

Maggie came in slower, looking around with big eyes before sitting in the recliner his dad always used.

If Rhodes cared, he didn't say so.

"Why are you here?" he asked, his tone even and calm.

He might have been calm; I was currently a nervous wreck. My insides were practically shaking from anxiety and anger.

Maggie crossed her legs demurely at the ankles. "Thank you for seeing me."

"Again, why exactly am I seeing you *now*?" Disdain dripped from his words.

She settled her hands in her lap. "I ... I needed to make sure you were okay after I heard about your father."

Rhodes went still. "How did you hear about that? Did Gabriel call you?"

She shook her head quickly, her dark hair swishing above her shoulders. "No, no. The facility did. You father and I spoke ... yesterday."

"Yesterday?" Rhodes repeated. "As in the day before he killed himself?"

She nodded, tears in her eyes. "Yes. One of the steps of his program was to," she sucked in a shuddering breath, "make amends."

"What could he possibly have to amend with *you*?" he snapped. "Last time I checked you did the leaving, *Mom*."

"He realized he had put unrealistic expectations on me and our marriage," she whispered. "It was why I left. I couldn't handle the pressure of being a wife and a mate and a ..."

"Mother?" he hissed. "You couldn't handle being a *mother*, right?"

"I was so young," she said brokenly. "I made a mistake. It's one that I deeply regret."

"You never came back!" he roared. "Maybe you made a mistake leaving, but you never bothered coming back!"

"Your father—"

"Forget my father," he cut her off. "What about *me*?"

Swallowing, Maggie looked down at her lap. Part of me was happy to see she was miserable.

But Rhodes was also miserable. And hurt.

That I couldn't stand.

I leaned harder against him and rested a hand on his rock-hard thigh, needing to reassure him I was still here. Still with him.

He relaxed the barest inch, but it was still there.

"I made a lot of mistakes, Rhodes. I know that. But I thought about you every day. Every day I was gone," she told him, her voice breaking and tears falling. "Every time I had worked up the nerve to call you or get in the car to see you … I didn't want to upset your life, baby. I knew you would be happier without me."

"Happier without a mom? Left alone to fend for myself while my dad sat in *that* chair and drank his life away?" Rhodes growled at her.

Maggie stayed quiet, tears sliding down her cheeks.

Rhodes sucked in a shaky breath, his body vibrating with barely contained energy and emotion.

"Why did you come here tonight?" I asked softly, finally breaking the heavy silence. I fixed my gaze on Maggie, not letting up. "What do you want?"

"To apologize," she whispered, wiping her eyes and looking at me like I was her last hope at getting through to her son.

I narrowed my eyes. No way was I taking her side over Rhodes *ever*.

"I just want Rhodes to realize I made a mistake," she told me, leaning forward. She glanced at him. "I … I remarried a couple years ago. If you need a place to live, you would be welcome in our pack. I already spoke to our Alpha."

"Not happening," I answered for Rhodes. "His family is *here*."

I felt the shaking of his shoulders as he chuckled under his breath. His hand slid from my shoulder to the back of my neck, massaging the tense skin there.

"I'm not leaving my pack," he affirmed. "Or Larkin."

Maggie nodded and sat back. "Of course. I just wanted you to know … You have the option. Anytime. My husband, Lee, never had any children. He said he would love to meet you. You could come and stay with us."

"Yeah, I'll have to think about that." His tone said he wouldn't give it another thought in this lifetime.

"Okay," she replied softly.

"So, did he make amends?" Rhodes asked suddenly.

Her expression softened. "For a while we talked about you. About how smart you are, how incredible you are, despite having us for parents. He was so proud of you, Rhodes. For being a beta. He mentioned you were a self-taught mechanic, too. Always managing to fix things. He knew he didn't deserve you as a son."

Maggie's face crumpled. "But then, he … he asked me to come home. Said we could all be family again. I told him I had remarried. That it couldn't happen. He said … he said he was happy for me. And then hung up." She drew in a ragged breath. "The center called me this morning after Gabriel. They told me what had happened. I knew I had to come see you."

Rhodes exhaled slowly. "Now you've seen me."

"Rhodes—"

"And now you can go," he said coldly.

She hunched her shoulders, hands shaking. "Honey, with your father dead, I wanted to invite you to come and live with me. I know you're technically an adult, but you're my son. My only child."

I stiffened, my gaze snapping to Rhodes. He looked completely blank, staring at a spot above Maggie's head.

Her desperate gaze swung to me. "Larkin, please."

"Rhodes told you to leave," I said softly, squaring my shoulders at the woman who had caused Rhodes so much hurt and pain and self-doubt. "But if you need me to physically show you the door, I will."

Maggie gasped but quickly scrambled to her feet. She dug through her purse and dropped a piece of paper on the table. "This is my phone number and address. Rhodes, honey, if you need anything—"

I grabbed the paper, crumpling it in my hand for him. "If we need you, we'll call."

She ducked her head with one last wobbly smile and then hurried out of the room. The front door shut a moment later. Within seconds, Remy and Skye were in front of us.

"Are you okay?" Remy asked.

"Can I kick her ass?" Skye demanded at the same time.

Remy gave her a look, and she rolled her eyes.

"Fine," she said, sitting down with a huff. "But the offer stands."

"Get in line," I muttered, tossing the paper back onto the table.

Rhodes got up and paced to the window, looking out at where the darkness was closing in.

"Rhodes?" Remy prompted.

"My dad killed himself after he talked to her," he explained woodenly. "Apparently he wanted his nonexistent happy family back, but Mom already has a new husband. If he couldn't have her ... then what was the point?"

I pressed my lips together, fighting back tears at the bitter rejection in his voice.

Because he wasn't enough to make his dad keep trying.

Remy sighed, shaking his head. "I'm sorry, man."

"It wasn't you, Rhodey," Skye told him. "None of this is on you. Not your mom, not your dad—"

He whirled around, pain bright in his eyes. "But I wasn't enough, was I, Skye? I wasn't enough for either of them to stay."

"That's *not on you*," she repeated firmly. "Trust me; I've seen my share of shitty choices and suicide. I've seen that moment when people give up."

Rhodes flinched at the reminder that Skye had grown up in the worst situation imaginable.

"When someone gets that hopeless, that lost in their own head, the only thing that can pull them out is their own will," she kept going vehemently. "People are responsible for their own choices. Their weakness, their faults—they aren't yours, Rhodes. People have to own their own shit."

Rhodes slowly nodded, raking a hand through his hair. "I need…"

"What?" Remy asked after he didn't finish the thought.

His eyes found mine and I knew. In that split second, I knew.

"I need to get out of here for a little while," he whispered.

A piece of my heart broke off, the serrated edges scraping out my insides even as I nodded.

"Pack a bag and come to my house," Remy said with a nod. "Get out of this house for a few days. Hell, don't come back. You know you can stay with me as long as you like."

"No," Rhodes said slowly, tearing his eyes from mine to look at Remy. "I need to get out of Blackwater. Just for a few days or something. I need to clear my head."

Remy looked ready to protest, but Skye grabbed his wrist.

"Are you sure?" she pressed.

Rhodes nodded. "Yeah. I just need to get away for a few days. Be on my own to sort shit out. Figure out what to do next."

"You can do that here," Remy argued. "We can leave. Give you space."

Rhodes spread his arms wide. "Look around, Rem. Everywhere I go in this house, there's a ghost around the corner. Every place in this town will have someone who will tell me they're sorry. Or ask if they can help. Or give me their pity."

Remy growled, rubbing the back of his neck viciously. "Rhodes—"

I got to my feet, walking over to Rhodes.

His dark eyes studied me, full of pain and confusion and love.

"Larkin." He framed my face in his hands.

I pressed my fingertips against his lips. "It's okay. Go clear your head. I'm here when you get back."

"You're sure?" he asked quietly, his thumb sweeping across the arch of my cheekbone.

"It's always been you, Rhodes," I said firmly, clearly, even as I wanted to curl up in a ball and sob my eyes out.

He leaned down, pressing his lips once, twice to mine. "It's always been you, baby girl."

He kissed me one last time, a deep, lingering kiss that I felt in my soul.

And then he was gone.

14

RHODES

I had been on the road for almost four days, not stopping except in a few motels to crash in the evenings, and only then because it was too cold to sleep in the old SUV I had inherited from my dad.

Wrapping my hands around the steering wheel, I grimaced.

The only gift he had ever given me.

Unless you counted that shot of whiskey he handed me on my thirteenth birthday.

I had driven east for a while, and then I cut north. Each day I stopped along a stretch of road, parking off to the side and shifting. Running had been my escape, my wolf keeping us running until we were both exhausted at night.

I ran several hours a day, the cold air helping to clear my head, the time with my wolf helping to center me.

But every time my paws touched the earth, every time I fell into bed at night, something was missing. Some*one* was missing.

Larkin.

Fuck, I missed her.

Glancing at the clock on the dash, I knew I was going to be pushing it on time if I wanted to be back at midnight.

Larkin's birthday party was supposed to start at eight, an annual tradition with her family and friends. At this rate, and with a new wave of snow starting to fall, I wouldn't make it before eleven.

As long as I got to kiss her when this year rolled into the next, that was all that mattered.

One thing the last four days had definitely helped drive into my brain was that the empty house I had grown up in wasn't my home. Larkin was. My friends were. The people who always had my back.

By now Dad would be in a box, a fragmented mess of ashes, but Dad had been fragmented and gone for a long time before now.

Maybe now he would find some actual peace.

Maybe we both would.

I turned the corner and almost missed the small compact that had slid off the side of the road, the flashers barely noticeable through the heavy curtain of snow.

I eased the truck onto the side of the road, throwing it in park and turning on my own flashers. I was about to reach in the glove box for a flashlight when a fist slammed against the passenger side window.

Wide, frantic gray eyes stared in at me, the man wildly gesturing to me.

I reached over, manually rolling down the window.

"Thank God," he said in a rush, his breath puffing out in white clouds as he breathed hard. "You gotta help us. Please. My wife. The car spun out. We have no cell reception. *My wife.*"

I was already getting out of the car. "Is your wife okay? Are you okay?" I dug my phone out of my pocket and checked. I didn't have cell service either.

I slid down the embankment towards the car, the man hot on my heels. I could hear the strangled groans and screams of a woman inside it. The fading light from the interior of the car only gave me a shadowed view of the woman in the backseat.

I yanked open the door and froze.

The man nudged me aside. "It's okay, sweetheart. I got us help. Let's get you into the car and to the hospital."

The woman gasped, clutching her very pregnant stomach, sweat slicking her hair down to her head. She shook her head violently.

"Can't. Baby's coming." She hissed out another breath, ending on a moan.

"No, no, no," the man argued, shaking his head. "We have to get you to the hospital. You can't have the baby *here*."

Her blue eyes flashed at him, clear despite the pain. "David, it's happening. *Now*. My contractions are only a few minutes apart and getting stronger. The baby is coming *now*."

David still seemed to be in shock. "But ... you can't."

Her eyes went to me. "Do you have a phone?"

"No service," I replied helplessly. "I'm Rhodes."

"Connie," she said through gritted teeth. "Rhodes, if you would be so kind as to slap my husband for me, maybe that will wake him up enough to help deliver his child?"

I grinned at her, leaning into the car. "This backseat is small. My SUV is bigger. You'd have more room?" If I folded the seats down, she would have a lot more space to ... have a baby.

I winced at the thought.

She nodded. "Thank you."

I sniffed the air on instinct, catching their scents, noting the subtle difference from normals.

"What pack are you from?" I asked.

David seemed to suddenly remember he was part of this conversation. "Corday," he replied, reaching into the car and helping his wife slide out. Her feet barely touched the snow before he had her lifted in his arms.

"There's blankets in the trunk and some bottled water—can you grab them?" he called over his shoulder.

I quickly gathered the supplies, following them up the slippery hill.

David already had Connie in the back of the truck. I opened the back door and laid the back seats flat so she had more room, dropping the blankets and water into the truck before going to the driver's side and getting in.

David met my eyes in the rearview mirror. "Keep heading down this road. The pack is about fifteen minutes away."

Connie groaned as another contraction hit. "We're not gonna make it."

"We'll try," David told her firmly, taking her hand in his and leaning between the two front seats, guiding me as I pulled back onto the road.

"You from around here?" Connie asked on a gasp.

"Um, not exactly. Passing through on my way home to Blackwater," I answered, trying to focus on the road that was becoming harder to see. No wonder their little car had gone off the road. I was in four-wheel drive and still having issues.

"Blackwater, huh? I hear that's a nice town," she said in a rushed breath.

"The talking helps distract her from the pain," David told me.

"Nothing distracts me from the pain," Connie retorted, but I heard the smile in her voice. "I just figure we should know the guy saving our asses. What are you doing out here?"

"I took a trip to clear my mind. My dad, um, died a few days ago."

"Crap, I'm sorry," Connie muttered, crying out again suddenly.

"Another contraction?" I asked, looking back at them and wondering if this much pain and gasping was normal.

No wonder there was a fertility issue amongst packs—what woman would willingly go through this pain multiple times?

"She's fine," David said, softly coaching her to remember to breathe.

Connie exhaled loudly. "Shit, that was a bad one."

"Are they supposed to be that bad?" I asked, worried.

"Yeah, from what I hear. At least this was fast. I only went into labor a few hours ago, so we thought we would have time to get home to the midwife," she explained, her breathing heavy and labored. "Usually labor lasts longer, though. Sometimes more than a day, but this guy can't wait to make an appearance."

I really should've paid more attention in health class.

"Turn right up ahead," David told me as Connie cried out again.

"They're getting closer together," she hissed when she caught her breath.

"I know, honey. We're almost there," he promised her.

God, I hoped he was right.

"So, Rhodes," she said again, her voice slightly weaker than before, "you still in school?"

"Uh, yeah." I glanced back at them. "I go to Granite Peak Academy."

"The school was set up by a group of packs, right? I hear it's great." Connie smiled at David. "Maybe this little guy will go there one day."

"If that's what you want," David told her, smiling softly down at her.

They were completely in love. This kid would have two parents who absolutely loved him and each other.

"Girlfriend?" Connie asked after another contraction.

The thought of Larkin was like a punch in a gut and stepping into sunshine all at once. God, I missed her.

"Yeah," I replied after a minute, swallowing down my emotions. "Her name is Larkin. She's my … she's everything."

David chuckled. "Yeah. I know how that goes. Just wait—a few years from now maybe you'll break down on the side of the road when she's in labor, too."

The idea of Larkin being pregnant didn't terrify me the way I expected it would.

Or should.

The idea of being a dad, especially with Larkin next to me, felt … right.

But no way in hell would I have Larkin's pregnant ass out on these roads.

"Next left," David called.

I took the turn slowly so we wouldn't slide, grateful as hell when I saw lights at the end of the road. I made it to the entrance, rolling down my window when I saw the men standing guard at a front gate.

Since females had started disappearing it seemed like

more and more packs had started patrolling their borders and using guarded entrances to pack lands.

I rolled my window down and David leaned forward.

"Owen! Hey!"

"David? That you?" The guard leaned into the open window, his eyes flicking to me warily.

"Our car broke down. Connie's in labor."

As if on cue, Connie cried out again.

Owen's eyes went huge and he waved us through. "I'll radio the med center and let them know you're coming!"

A few more turns down small, unpaved roads, and I was pulling up in front of a crudely constructed house. A man and woman rushed out, throwing open the doors.

"Rhodes, thank you," David called, climbing out of the back and lifting a groaning Connie into his arms. "I owe you."

"Thank you!" Connie cried out, eyes squeezed shut against the pain. She offered a limp wave over her mate's shoulder as he carried her to the medical clinic.

The doors of the truck slammed shut and I was left in sudden, stark silence. Giving myself a mental shake, I checked the clock again.

Shit. I would definitely be pushing it to make it before midnight now.

Putting the SUV back in drive I headed out of the compound, rolling through the guard station and turning back onto the main road, praying I would make it in time.

☪

Larkin

My eyes drifted to the clock for the fifteenth time in the last ten minutes. I had no idea how time was simultaneously flying and crawling.

My mom came up and wrapped an arm around me, enveloping me in the fragrance of lilies. It was a soft scent that my mind automatically knew and clung to.

"There's still time, love," she whispered in my ear. "He'll be here."

I nodded, unable to speak as I watched the room full of people laughing and joking, the giant TV over the fireplace turned on to the local New Year's countdown.

Eleven minutes left until the New Year began.

Until my birthday.

It was stupid, but I wanted to start the New Year with Rhodes. With his lips on mine, ready to tackle this new year together.

We hadn't spoken since he left. I lost track of how many times I almost called him. Almost texted. But I knew he needed time, had asked for time, and I wanted to give him that.

I had told my mom everything the minute they came home, sitting in my bed, crying into my pillow about almost everything. She listened patiently, calmly. She knew I had loved Rhodes for years, seen how crushed I was when he went out on dates with other girls or told people I was like his sister.

I don't think I would have left my bed the last four days if not for my parents, Skye, and Katy all keeping me occupied.

Clearing my throat, I gave her a weak smile. "I need to go to the bathroom."

She nodded slowly, her gaze missing absolutely nothing as she let me go. "Go on. I'll get the cake ready."

Tradition had me blowing out the candles at midnight while everyone cheered around me. Usually it was my favorite part of the whole party, but I would have given anything to simply go upstairs and sleep through this night.

I headed down the hallway to the powder room, stepping inside and hitting the light. As I was shutting the door, a hand slammed against it, stopping me.

My heart leaped. I spun around, sagging when I saw it was Katy and Skye behind me, not Rhodes.

Katy gave me a serious look. "In ten minutes, it's going to be your birthday and the start of a whole new year. And I know you wanted him here, but it doesn't change the fact that you're in a houseful of people who love you and want to celebrate you."

I sighed and let them into the small space with me, turning to brace my hands on the sink and looking at myself in the mirror.

Katy and Skye had come over and helped me get ready. My dark hair was curled in loose waves, falling around my shoulder like a shiny, dark curtain. Katy had done my makeup, a simple black winged liner that made my eyes smoky and crimson lipstick that matched the red of the dress I had picked out months ago for this party.

Because Rhodes loved red.

"I thought he would be here," I whispered, dropping my eyes and willing myself not to cry.

Skye wrapped an arm around my waist as Katy looped an arm over my shoulders. They rested their heads on my shoulders.

"I'm sorry," Skye said gently, "but he's coming back. You know that."

"I know," I replied, sniffling and blinking hard against the hot rush of tears. I tipped my head back, exhaling a shaky breath.

"Let's go blow out your candles and eat a crap ton of cake and ice cream," Katy suggested. "Skye and I will even spend the night and we can watch crappy rom-coms."

Skye smiled, nodding encouragingly, tucking a piece of hair behind my ear.

Squaring my shoulders, I gave my reflection a decisive nod and took a steadying breath.

"Okay, let's do this."

The lights in the main room had been turned off and I could see the candlelight from the cake flickering as we made our way down the hallway. I paused in the doorway, my eyes sweeping the room and seeing the faces of my family and friends. They all smiled, most have no idea my heart was a gaping wound as they started singing *Happy Birthday*.

Skye and Katy stayed close to me as I bent over the massive cake and took a deep breath.

"Make a wish!" Someone yelled in the crowd.

I made the same wish I had been making for the last four days.

I blew out the candles, opening my eyes to make sure I got them all in one breath just as the announcer on the TV yelled, "Happy New Year!"

The room exploded into pandemonium. Couples hugged and kissed, friends high-fived and hugged. My parents each hugged me before kissing each other. Remy snagged Skye around the waist, kissing her soundly.

I stepped back, closing my eyes to the images of all these stupidly happy people, and bumped into the wall.

Hands settled on my hips, steadying me.

Not a wall.

My heart stopped, time slowing down.

"Happy birthday, baby girl," Rhodes whispered in my ear.

15

RHODES

I LOST COUNT OF HOW MANY TIMES I ALMOST SLID OFF THE road, definitely going faster than I probably should have, but it was worth it to make it in time for this.

Larkin trembled against me, shaking under my touch as I whispered in her ear, "Happy birthday, baby girl."

With a gasp, she spun and launched herself at me. I fell back into the wall with a chuckle, as Larkin wrapped her arms and legs around me, burying her face in my neck and inhaling deeply.

I lifted her higher in my arms, loving the feel of her pressed against me. Closing my eyes, I breathed her in, the familiar scent of strawberries filling my senses. My wolf sighed happily, at peace now that she was with us again.

She lifted her head, tears sparkling in her eyes as she touched my face. "I didn't think you would make it," she admitted, choking on the words.

"I almost didn't," I admitted. "It's a long story I'll tell you all about it."

A gorgeous smile stretched across her face, her nose brushing mine as her eyes sparkled in the low lighting.

"I missed you," she told me quietly.

"I missed you, too," I answered, pressing my lips to hers. Like always, the second her mouth touched mine, fire ignited.

Her legs tightened around my waist and I had to remember we were in a room full of people before I spun her around and pressed her against the wall.

My lips caressed hers, my tongue slowly stroking into her mouth as I relearned her taste all over again.

A throat cleared behind me and I reluctantly broke the kiss, looking over to see a room full of people watching us.

I let Larkin go, biting back a groan as she slid down my body, intentionally rubbing against me despite her parents standing a few feet away and obviously watching us.

The second Larkin stepped away, her mom was there, pulling me into a hug.

"I'm so sorry about your father, honey," she whispered, her arms tight around me as she squeezed hard.

Larkin's dad offered his hand to me next, shaking mine firmly. "If you need anything, you let us know. You're family, kid."

I barely had time to smile at him before Katy and Skye were hugging me, followed by Remy and his parents. Several others offered their condolences about my dad, and it didn't bother me the way I expected.

It felt … nice. Comforting to have my pack surround me.

Larkin took my hand. "Mom, Dad, we're going to—"

"Stay here to hang out with everyone who came to celebrate your birthday? Open that mountain of presents in the corner?" her dad interrupted, lifting an eyebrow.

Larkin sighed, her head drooping slightly as she forced a smile. "Of course."

"I'm teasing, sweetheart. You two go. We know you have a lot to talk about," he told her, smiling indulgently.

She reached up and hugged him quickly with one arm, still holding me with the other.

"Thank you," I told him sincerely. I had wondered if Larkin and I being together would make things awkward with her parents, but clearly it hadn't.

There were people all over Larkin's house, so I led her out the back door and towards my house, opening the back door for her. After a few sliding steps in her heels, I picked her up and carried her the rest of the way, not stopping until we were inside my house. I kicked the door shut with my foot, setting her on the countertop and stepping between her legs.

"Lark—"

She cut me off by kissing me, hooking her ankles low around my back and pulling me flush against her. I groaned into her mouth, my hands coming up to cradle her face and angle her mouth where I could best devour her.

Grinding her center against me, I reached down, sliding a hand under the skirt of her dress and up her thigh until I reached her damp center.

"Fuck," I swore, tearing my mouth from hers as I pushed her panties aside and easily slid a finger into her.

Her head fell back against the cabinets with a thud.

"Ow," she said with a laugh, reaching up to rub the back of her head.

"Be careful," I murmured, one hand going around to cradle the back of her head while I added a second finger.

"Rhodes, please," she whimpered, her hands pulling at the jacket I still had on, her hips jerking against my hand.

I withdrew my hand, licking my fingers clean and watching her eyes widen, her breathing getting harder.

Reaching behind her, I undid the zipper of her dress, helping her slide it off her body. I barely registered the black lace strapless bra, quickly divesting her of it before I jerked her panties off her body.

It only took me a matter of seconds to strip out of my clothes.

She lifted a leg to remove her heels and I grabbed her ankle.

"Leave those," I said, my voice deep and rough as I smoothed the pad of my thumb across the delicate straps.

I tugged her hips to the edge and was inside her in a single, deep thrust that had her crying out.

"Too much?" I asked, chest heaving as I resisted the urge to fuck her as hard as I could.

She wrapped her legs around me once more, the points of her heels digging into my ass.

"No," she managed, grabbing my shoulders. "More."

I pumped into her in long, deep strokes until I felt her body start to convulse around mine, her pussy clenching hard around me, driving me over the edge with a roar.

I held her in my arms for several quiet minutes, our racing hearts settling, her body wrapped around mine.

"Are you okay?" she asked, pulling back to look me in the eye. "Did you clear your head? Figure things out?"

Sighing, I pressed my forehead to hers. "Yeah. I think I got it all figured out."

"Is there anything you need?" God, she was so sweet and selfless.

And mine.

"Yeah," I answered softly. "I could use a tutor."

Her tiny nose wrinkled. "A tutor?"

"I need to get my grades up if I want to apply to college," I told her with a small smile.

Her eyes went round, her mouth dropping open. "You're going to college?"

"I was thinking maybe a business degree would be a good idea if I want to open my own garage," I replied.

"I think that's a great idea," she whispered, tears in her eyes again.

"On one condition." I held up a finger.

She grinned. "Name it."

Smirking, I leaned in and told her, "You have to join a sorority."

Laughing, she pulled her head back. "So, you can still screw sorority girls?"

"Only one," I corrected with a smile.

"You know if I join a sorority I'll probably live in the sorority house. Not with you in the pack housing."

"Fuck that. I'll buy you a sorority jacket or sweater or whatever, and you can wear it when I want to screw a sorority chick."

She giggled harder. "Got it all figured out, huh?"

I sobered, lifting a hand to her face. "No, I don't. But I know I have you, and you have me. The rest we can figure out as we go along."

"You've always had me," she replied honestly, gently. "And you always will."

"It's always been you," I murmured, kissing her slowly.

It would always be her.

COMING SOON

Remy & Skye will return Winter 2021
   PREY (Blackwater Pack #2)
   By: Hannah McBride

Keep reading for the first 2 chapters!

PREY

Chapter 1

"Stop!" I gasped the word out suddenly, my body tense and tight as pain arced through me.

Holy hell, that hurt. Was it supposed to hurt *that* much? Clearly we were doing this wrong.

Remy grimaced above me, his muscles shaking as he tried to hold back. "Stopping right now isn't exactly an option, babe."

I glared up at him, my jaw clenched. "Well, this hurts, so make it an option, Remy."

His dark gaze narrowed. "I *know*. I told you it probably would the first few times."

"You didn't mention *this* much hurt," I snapped, ready to call it quits now. My body shook with exhaustion, my chest heaving.

Remy sighed, his head dropping and nearly touching my shoulder. "Skye, you can't just yell, 'stop' in the middle of a fight and think the person trying to kill you will decide to take a time out."

Now I glared at him, resisting the urge to turn my head and bite his wrist where he had my arm pinned down.

But it would have been seriously childish ... and there was no way Remy would've allowed it. He was too fast, too smart, and too good a fighter to let that happen.

My boyfriend was definitely a badass when it came to all things shifter and fighting related. I assumed it came with the alpha-to-be territory, but when I had asked him to start teaching me some self-defense moves, I didn't realize I was signing up for Remington Holt Boot Camp: Extreme Shifter Edition.

I thought it would be a good way to take back a piece of my self esteem that Cassian had stolen when he kidnapped me or spent years torturing me. I had been powerless then, but I wasn't anymore.

Except right now? I kinda was.

Remy took his role as teacher very seriously, as seriously as he took my safety, which had gone from high-alert to DEFCON-5 after my abduction. He was my alpha and my mate. One would have been enough to become obsessed with my safety, but both meant he wasn't cutting me any slack on learning to protect myself.

I could see the moment he decided to call it a day, and I rejoiced even though my wolf was pissed off he had bested us at least ten times in a row.

But maybe we can both still win.

I wrapped my legs around his waist, using my lower body strength to pull him down on top of me, fitting our bodies together. Caught off guard, he fell into me, his nose brushing mine.

Remy arched a single brow slowly, glancing down at where my legs were locked around him. His heated gaze moved to my eyes, his already dark eyes getting even darker.

"While this may be a good distraction tactic," he allowed in a rough voice, "I don't think I'm a fan of you using this particular technique on anyone else."

His hands still had mine pinned by my head.

"Only you," I said softly, my gaze flickering to his mouth, my eyes pleaded for him to close the inch between our lips.

He didn't disappoint.

His lips closed over mine, his tongue sweeping inside my mouth open as he deepened the kiss. I wriggled under him, wanting my hands free to pull him closer, but he held me down. I felt his lips curve into a wicked smile against mine as he kept kissing me.

With a gasp, I arched my neck, his lips trailing down my jaw and leaving wet kisses along the column of my throat.

My legs squeezed harder around his waist, my body igniting as he held me in place, taking his time kissing me. Leaving me powerless to do anything except take what he was giving.

The front door opened behind us.

"This doesn't *look* like teaching self-defense," Rhodes said with a smirk as he strolled in and stopped beside us. "At least, this is never how we sparred, Rem."

With a grumble, Remy stood up, pulling me with him. My body pressed against his for a single delicious second that ended way too soon. With a low groan, he headed for the kitchen to grab our waters while I slapped Rhodes on the arm.

"Great timing," I muttered.

He shrugged innocently. "Maybe you two need to be properly chaperoned from now on."

Remy flipped him off while handing me my bottle.

I arched a brow at Rhodes. "And where are you coming from exactly?" His hair definitely hadn't been that mussed when he left here a few hours earlier, and his shirt wasn't nearly as wrinkled.

A smug grin drifted across his face. "Larkin was helping me study."

Remy rolled his eyes. "Studying, right."

"Do I even want to know what you were studying?" I asked with a smirk, taking a long drink of the cold water.

His grin deepened. "Chemistry, of course." He winked. "I'm acing that class."

"Of course," I echoed with a snort. "And now you're done studying?"

Rhodes frowned. "Lark kicked me out. Something about needing to *actually* study."

That sounded more like my best friend. I laughed, turning away from them both and heading for the stairs. "I'm taking a shower before dinner."

I hurried up the stairs and went into my room, closing the door as I stripped out of my work out clothes, tossing them across the perfectly made bed.

It was hard to mess up a bed I never slept in.

I had taken Remy up on his offer to move into the alpha cabin when we returned the school a day earlier, with the provision that I got the guest room next to his room as my own.

I wasn't quite ready to *move in*-move in with him yet.

But of course last night I slept in his bed our first night back on campus. We had only slept.

After him spending almost every night with me over winter break, I wasn't ready to lose that. Especially now that we were back at GPA. The last time I had been here, I nearly died.

A shudder wracked my frame, and I squeezed my eyes shut, trying to shove away the memory of waking up on the side of a mountain after Cassian had drugged and kidnapped me. I tried to ignore the memories of fighting with him and going over the cliff.

Parts of my memory were still broken, but I had dreams about falling, my body breaking against the hard ground at the bottom of the cliff. Sometimes Cassian was in my dreams, still alive, and he succeeded in taking me back to Long Mesa.

In the worst nightmares, it was Remy who went over the edge with Cassian. Remy's body that smashed against the gray stones and dead leaves.

Those dreams killed me. I would wake up screaming and sobbing. The first time I had that particular nightmare was right after Christmas. Mom had come running into my room, finally calling Remy and making him come to the apartment at two in the morning when I couldn't calm down.

I didn't stop crying and shaking until I saw he was okay for myself.

After that, he used the tree outside my window to sneak into my room every night over break. When the nightmares were bad, it helped waking up to see him next to me. Sometimes he felt me slipping into them before I knew what it was, and he could talk me out of them. I would wake up, wrapped tightly in his arms, his lips whispering against my ear.

I was worried being back in the place I had last seen Cassian would trigger a nightmare last night, but I had slept soundly through the night.

Giving the bed one last look, I sighed and went into the bathroom. Odds are I wouldn't be sleeping in that bed anytime soon.

I heard the shower in Remy's bathroom kick on as I was turning my shower off and stepping out. It took me hardly any time to towel off my hair and body and get dressed. I quickly braided my dark hair, leaving it wet despite the Montana winter outside.

A few months ago I had learned I hated hair dryers.

The blast of hot air felt too much like the New Mexico desert, and pack, I had left behind.

If leaving my hair wet meant I didn't get that split second flashback, I would deal with it. Even if the Montana air was hovering at a crisp eleven degrees.

Rhodes was playing a video game when I came back downstairs. I glanced at the clock on the cable box, noting we only had fifteen minutes until dinner would be served in the cafeteria of the main building.

"How was it out there?" I asked, sitting on the other end of the couch.

"Like a ghost town," he replied.

After last semester, half the packs that attended Granite Peak Academy decided not to return, leaving the campus feeling really empty and a little creepy. Half the alpha cabins around the property sat empty and dark, just empty shells where people used to live.

Rhodes still lived in the alpha house with Remy, and now me, but hardly anyone else shared a room on campus now. There was enough space for everyone to have their own rooms in the dorms for the first time in years, and most people seemed to love that.

Rhodes offered to stay in the dorms (okay, his first choice

was one of the leftover alpha cabins with Larkin), but I hated the idea of displacing him from the place he had lived since he started GPA as a freshman. Plus, his dad had just died, and he needed his best friend. Breaking up Remy and Rhodes was never an option.

Besides, it took some of the pressure off of my relationship with Remy. A relationship that was still firmly ranked as PG-13, to my growing frustration.

Remy knew my history with my first pack, and my complicated, often volatile, past with male shifters. He never wanted me to feel pressured in any way about our bond or the pace I moved at.

But my wolf and I were both a little tired of the lack of action. Not that there had been much time to do … *things* over winter break. Remy and I had missed the last part of the fall semester and spent most of our break catching up so we could still graduate in the Spring. Plus, we applied to college, Remy helped his dad with the pack, and I even started working part time at the cafe with my mom.

And at night … Well, nothing said sexy-times like a girl who was terrified of turning the lights out and prone to shriek-inducing nightmares. Remy was usually more focused on making me relaxed at night; not on activities that would have the opposite effect.

Classes started tomorrow, so hopefully having that routine would help normalize things, even if the campus was eerily absent of half the students that had been there only a few weeks earlier.

I personally was all for the emptier campus if it meant Trace, the Norwood pack, and their allies were all far away.

After attacking Larkin at the dance, breaking Katy's leg, and bringing Cassian to the school, I never needed to see

Trace again. He had made it his mission to destroy my pack and my mate.

I knew Remy was still pissed there was unfinished business between them (mostly that Trace ran away while Remy was sitting vigil by my hospital bed before Remy could kick his ass), but I was looking forward to a much more relaxed final semester of high school and started college.

I watched Rhodes kick ass on the TV for a few minutes until Remy came downstairs in a pair of jeans that hung low on his hips, tugging his shirt down over his abs.

"You're drooling," Rhodes murmured beside me.

I kicked at him with my foot. "Jerk."

Remy walked behind the couch on his way to get his boots, smacking the back of Rhodes' head as he went.

"Hey!" Rhodes yelped, grabbing the back of his head. "What did I do?"

"Whatever you did to make Skye kick you," he retorted with a grin.

I gave him a smug look, standing up to go get my own shoes. Rhodes turned off the game and the TV, getting up as well.

I slipped my arms into my jacket as Remy pulled a knit beanie over my head, flicking the ends of my braid. "You're going to freeze."

With a shrug, I ducked past him and opened the front door to go outside.

The path that led to the main building was barely clear and snow was still falling. I quickly descended the stairs, tipping my face up to catch snowflakes on my face. I loved the fluffy white stuff.

Remy came up behind me silently, his footsteps muffled by the snow. But it didn't matter. I could sense him behind me, near me. I could always sense where he was, even when he was out of sight.

If my heart was a compass, Remy Holt was my true North.

Probably another side effect of the mate bond we shared, but it gave me a certain level of comfort, especially when I couldn't see him with my own eyes.

He slid his arms around my waist, pulling my back flush to his chest, lighting up nerve endings through layers of clothes and coats.

The tip of his warm nose brushed my jaw a second before his lips ghosted over the same spot. "Let's go."

His gloved hand closed over mine and he tugged me down the path. I watched the snow falling around us as he and Rhodes talked about some new game they both wanted when it came out in a few months. As we got closer to the building, I could see more students heading the same way.

My shoulders stiffened when I realized they kept glancing over at us.

"Why are people looking at us?" I finally asked in a low voice when a group of guys stared and started talking quickly to each other as they ducked into the building.

Rhodes threw an arm across my shoulders. "You're famous, babe."

With a low growl, Remy pushed his arm off of me, hauling me to his side in a show of possessive male dominance that shouldn't have turned my insides to jelly the way it did, and probably broke a few laws of feminism.

Katy would be so disappointed.

Rhodes never stopped smiling, not phased in the least by his best friend going all alpha-caveman.

"Famous?" I echoed, slowing my steps. "What do you

mean?"

Brow furrowed, Rhodes slowed with me, looking first at me and then at Remy. "Not only did you end up in a coma after a showdown with a pack of alphas, but you and Remy are bonded. That *never* happens to shifters our age."

The mates part I could deal with, but the other …

I stopped altogether. "Do they know … who I am?"

Remy looked down at me before jerking his head for Rhodes to keep going. I could tell he wanted to reach for me, it was in his eyes, but we both knew I wanted answers more than I wanted comfort.

At least, right this second.

He took a deep breath. "They know what pack you're from. They know you're the niece of an Alpha, the granddaughter of an Alpha. They know who your mother is."

I winced at that. My mother basically started a war between the southern packs when she turned up pregnant a week before her marriage of alliance to another pack. Needless to say, the treaty was broken and it caused a massive wave of fallout that was fairly legendary in the shifter world.

"But they don't know the details about what happened in Long Mesa," he finished softly, his dark eyes concerned and fierce at the same time. "That's your story to tell when, and if, you want to, babe."

Logically I knew nothing that happened in Long Mesa was my fault. I never asked to grow up in a house where omegas were repeatedly abused on a daily basis. A house where I knew I would one day suffer the same fate.

I never asked for Cassian, Preston, and Marc to bully and harass me, finding ways to grope, grab, and intimidate me for years before Mom and I escaped.

And I sure as hell didn't ask Cassian to come to Granite

Peak last year or to kidnap me.

But it didn't mean I felt the shame any less. That gut-churning, black hole pit in my stomach that loomed wide, ready to devour me in humiliation when I remembered every minute of my past.

Remy leaned his forehead against mine, his skin shockingly warm despite the cold. "That life is over, babe. No one will ever touch you again."

I wound my arms around his neck. "Except you."

"Except me," he agreed, his voice a deep rumble I felt down to my toes as second before his soft lips descended on mine, coaxing my lips open to deepen the kiss.

I rolled to the balls of my feet, my arms tightening around him. I hated these puffy layers between us, the gloves on my hands that kept me from sliding my fingers through his hair and along his strong jaw.

His hands found my hips, his arms banding around me as he almost lifted me off the ground.

A series of giggles burst through the air behind us, snapping us out of our impromptu-makeout session.

Remy set me down, pulling away as our three younger female pack members looked at us with freaking stars in their eyes.

I couldn't even be mad. Lea, Bethany, and Megan had turned into the little sisters I never knew I wanted. I had even hung out with them a few times during break when Ainsley—freaking Ainsley who a few months ago hated me—had all of us over to her house for a slumber party one night.

But the three younger girls had quizzed me in every way they could think of about my bond with Remy until Katy and Ainsley told them to shut up and leave me alone.

I waved a gloved hand to them, and they waved back.

Remy followed my look with a smile. "Your fan club, huh?"

I snorted as we started for the doors. "Please. More like *your* fan club." I gave him a serious look. "Megan definitely has a thing for you."

He exhaled loudly, opening the door for me. "Too bad for Megan. I'm taken."

I whirled around with a shocked gasp. "Taken? Remington Holt has a girlfriend?"

He grinned, shaking his head at me. "I am *definitely* off the market."

"So, it's serious?" I teased, biting my lower lip.

His arm reached out, snagging me by the waist and pulling me into him. His dark eyes were liquid chocolate, warm and soft, as he looked down at me. "I love her completely."

I smiled up at him, my heart soaring in my chest. "The feeling is entirely mutual."

☪

Chapter 2

The cafeteria was barely half full when we walked inside.

Most students sat where they had before half of our classmates went to the darkside and didn't return, but conversations were hushed. There was a heaviness to the overall atmosphere around us, a strange prickling of awareness that things were different.

Even at our tables, where Rhodes and Ryder were usually joking around and being loud, were subdued.

Remy and I had been the last ones at our table. Larkin,

Rhodes, and Katy were already sitting in their usual spots, but this time there was a lot less room between Larkin and Rhodes than a few months ago.

Dante had brought part of the Brooks Ridge pack to our table. Tate sat between him and Ryder. She and Ryder grinned at me while Dante did that stoic nod that was all him.

I frowned, realizing someone was missing.

"Where's Maren?" I asked as I sat down next to Katy. Remy brushed his fingers across the back of my neck as he went to the line to grab our dinners.

Because I had a boyfriend who did things like get me dinner.

I squashed a stupid, completely girly giggle at the thought.

"Her grandmother died," Katy said softly, her lips turned down. "She stayed back for another week to be with her family."

Katy and Maren were inseparable at school, taking the crowns for PDA Queen and Queen. Katy had even gone up to Alaska during winter break to spend time with Maren, no small feat since the Brooks Ridge pack was a small town in Northern Alaska and planes rarely flew in and out. I knew they were both dreading the impending graduation where they would have to figure out where their relationship stood and if one wanted to move to the other's pack.

"I offered to stay with her," Tate added, "but she said she just wanted to spend time with her grandfather. They had been mates for over sixty years, so he's really struggling."

"Were they bonded?" I asked, sad for their loss.

Tate shook her head. "No."

Still, it couldn't be easy to lose someone you spent over

sixty *years* with. I had only been with Remy a few months and the idea of losing him...

I barely reigned in my wolf before she had us jumping up and touching him to make sure he was safe and sound. She whined at me, wanting her mate and I couldn't fault her for it, but I was getting a little concerned how attached I was getting to Remy.

I knew our bond enhanced a lot of things, but I didn't know of any bonded shifters who felt compelled to be with their mate twenty-four/seven.

Now that we were back at school, I planned to find Elias and talk to him. The old shifter was insanely knowledgeable about all things in the shifter world, including the true mate bond. He had spent his life collecting information about our kind and even had some kind of medical degree.

He had been working on formulating an idea for why the birth rate of shifters was steadily declining, but I was hoping he could give me insight into this sudden need to be with Remy all the time. He had helped me find out why I struggled with shifting, so maybe he could help me understand my wolf a little bit better.

I let out a slow breath as Remy finally returned, sliding a tray of pasta and salad in front of me before sitting in the vacant chair to my left. Stomach growling, I dug into the carbs first with my fork, my left hand reaching out to touch his thigh under the table, needing that reassurance he was here.

He didn't give me a weird look or even break the conversation he had started with Dante. He simply slid his hand over mine and squeezed my fingers.

That small, simple action relaxed me enough to focus on what was happening around me.

Which was, of course, about the packs who left.

"It will definitely make this year less stressful," Larkin was saying.

"But the whole point of the school was to show packs *could* work together," Dante reminded her, his deep voice sounding tired. "Half the packs leaving shows that a lot of these old divides are still holding true and strong."

"The divides will always be there. The alliances are what will help us. Now we know which packs we can't, and shouldn't align with," Rhodes mentioned, taking a slow drink. His dark eyes were thoughtful, reminding me there was a reason he was Remy's beta, his second in command. "But this school wasn't a failure."

Rhodes was a jokester and loved to laugh and have fun, but there was also an intensity to him and a mind that missed nothing.

Rhodes guestered around the room. "For years, Blackwater and Brooks Ridge could only count on each other. Now we've more than quadrupled our numbers. Yeah, we lost five packs, but we have seven here. *That* part worked. Every shifter in this room is part of a pack that stands with us."

Remy let out a low breath. "You're right. And they're numbers we're going to need going into the Summit."

"You mean votes," Katy muttered darkly. She flipped her long red hair over a shoulder with a glower. "Amazing the year we live in and *normals* have more rights than us."

Tate leaned back in her chair, her eyes bright. "She's right. It's ridiculous that the entire Summit is run by males trying to solve a *female* problem."

Dante reached over and cupped the back of her neck, making her look at him. "We're not saying you shouldn't have a say, sweetheart. You know everyone at this table, hell, every pack in this *room* agrees females should have more of a say. We're fighting for that."

Her hand came up to his jaw. "I *do* know that, but *you* don't know what it's like to sit back and have to wait for someone else to fight for you."

"Or not bother fighting at all," I added quietly, suddenly done with my meal. I set my fork down, opting to chew my lower lip instead.

Remy's arm was around my shoulders, tucking me into his side, before I even finished my statement. His lips found the side of my head. Now it seemed like *he* was the one reassuring himself I was still here.

"Your pack was a bunch of assholes," Ryder spat. "What they did…" He trailed off, shaking his head.

"Has there been any word about them making waves at the Summit?" Dante asked Remy.

Remy nodded firmly, his jaw set. "Nothing concrete, but it's coming. Odds are they're lining up their allies the same way we are."

"And they definitely aren't the only ones who think females should be … *controlled*." Katy's lips curled in disgust around the last word.

"Look at what happened to Skye," Tate agreed. "To *me*. Females are becoming some … commodity to be used for breeding rights and then, if we're lucky, sent to live out our days quietly like good little shifters. Females who can't—"

"—or *won't*," Katy cut in.

"Or won't," Tate added with a nod, "do their proverbial part, are shunned or banished from most packs."

"In Long Mesa they were forced to mate," I said slowly. My packmates knew this. I had shared with them, and Tate, about what happened to lesbian shifters or shifters who couldn't reproduce or refused to take a male mate. But from the horror on Dante and Ryder's, Tate hadn't shared those details.

"*Forced?*" Ryder choked out, coughing hard as the food he was chewing caught in his throat.

"Yeah, and Long Mesa wasn't the only pack that thought that way," I answered honestly. "Females are supposed to produce a child, either by choice or by force."

Both guys looked ready to drive down to my old pack and kick some ass after a trip to the bathroom to vomit all the food they had just eaten. I didn't bother adding that frequently those forced matings included multiple males to 'increase the likelihood of conception'.

And that it also happened in public. A warning of sorts to other females.

Katy slammed a small fist on the table. "See? This is the shit females have to deal with, and we get *zero* say in what happens to us. We just happened to luck out that our packs believe in equal rights. But even with the packs we're aligned with, we're still the minority."

"But, historically speaking, women did get the right to vote," Ryder added. "They got all sorts of rights."

"After centuries of oppression," Katy snapped. "So you're saying we should just sit back and wait for the Shifter B. Anthony to take up arms?"

"They also weren't dealing with their species dying off," Larkin chimed in softly, tucking a lock of dark hair behind her ear. "Females are becoming increasingly rare. Four males are born to every one female. It makes sense that the males would want to control the limited population there is and figure out the best way to keep the shifter population from dying out."

Katy opened her mouth, and Larkin held up a hand to silence her.

"I'm not saying it's right," she added quickly, "but it's where we are. Entire packs have died out. But now, a lot of Alphas are making decisions based on fear. Fear of their pack numbers dwindling, pack lineages ending... Until they start looking at this objectively, we're stuck in a cycle no one will break."

Rhodes lifted a hand after a second of silence. "I vote Larkin for President."

We all laughed. It was the break in seriousness we needed, something crack the tension that had us all wound up.

With a roll of her eyes, Larkin swatted a hand at him that he simply caught and pressed to his mouth. I smiled watching Larkin's eyes go soft, watching as Rhodes tugged her mouth to his next.

My friends were happy.

The fact that I could use the words 'friends' and 'happy' in the same sentence was a testament to how far I had come in the last few months.

As if sensing my mood, Remy nuzzled his nose against my neck. I bit back a giggle at the way it tickled when he breathed deeply against me.

"You guys seriously *suck*," Katy griped, but she was smiling under her glare. She was happy that her friends were happy.

The world might be chaos around us, but here, in this space, we were safe and we were together.

Which is of course when a scream rose up from the hallway that had every single shifter in the room jumped to their feet as a girl with pale hair ran frantically into the room.

She looked around with wild eyes until she spotted who she was looking for, her face crumpling.

I vaguely placed her as a shifter from the Dubonne pack in Michigan.

She never broke stride as she ran full speed at their pack campus alpha, who was now standing with his pack. He caught the girl in his arms.

"Jane, whoa, hey!" His arms banded around her, his eyes lifting to survey the room. I watched them land on each pack alpha. The other six alphas in the room, Remy and Dante leading the way, went and joined them.

The rest of us crowded close, but Jane seemed too damn hysterical to make much sense. She clung to her alpha—again, I *really* needed to learn the names of our allies—and trembled.

"Jane," he finally said, taking her by the shoulders and pushing her back a step. He only had a few inches on her and was definitely one of the younger alphas on campus. "Jane, you need to tell us what happened."

"She's gone!" Jane wailed, her head dropping forward.

A hushed murmur rose up amongst the shifters and I noticed the faculty joining the gathering.

"What do you mean *gone?*" the Dubonne alpha's tone shifted subtly, but definitely enough to know he was giving an alpha command to his pack member.

Wiping her eyes and nose, Jane looked helplessly at him. "Kit. She's *gone.*"

Preorder PREY now on Amazon
Available in paperback and KU on Jan. 8, 2021

ACKNOWLEDGMENTS

Here we go again.

As I'm writing this, I just realized it's been a year since I finished this book. And in that year, I've now published two books. Which is ... crazy pants.

First, foremost, and always, thank you to my Heavenly Father for giving me the ability and creativity to share stories with the world.

This book wouldn't have happened without 3 women who demanded to know more about Rhodes and Larkin, and begged for their story.

Krista Davis, I would be lost without you. Thank you for holding me hand through many parts of this book, and championing for Rhodes and Larkin from the start. I honestly couldn't have ever hoped for a better best friend to talk beside me in life.

Val Fink and Jess Baker: This wouldn't have happened without your support and love and harassing. Thank you for believing in me, encouraging me, and kicking my butt when I needed it. I love you, girls, so much. I owe you all the things.

Massive thanks to **Vonetta Young**, my unofficial PA; kinda-official bodyguard, and official lifelong friend. You push me every day to be the best version of myself as a person and a writer, and I love you for that. (Also thanks for sharing Alyna with me on our weekly calls.)

Thank you to my pack on Facebook: Asis Gonzalez, Lisa Carina Gaibler, Tracy Kirby, Jennifer Edwards Whiteoak, Kayleigh Gore, Katie Akers, Emily Bright, Chris Ann Simek, Nicole Sanchez, and the rest of the Blackwater Pack group.

My amazing friends who volunteered to help me edit this book: Kelly Wilmer & Chris La Forest. Thank you isn't enough.

Thank you to the authors who have inspired me and let me pick their brains about books and publishing: Elle Christensen, Alex Grayson, and Jennifer Armentrout; your guidance has been lifesaving.

Always thank you to my family: Mom, Dad, Sherry, Micah, and Lauren; Aunt Patti, Aunt Tina, Missi, and Gabrielle. Your support means the world to me.

To my favorite girls in the entire universe: Aria & Nora, I love you more than I will ever be able to put into words.

If you're reading this book, THANK YOU. From the absolute bottom of my heart, thank you.

ABOUT THE AUTHOR

Hannah McBride has been many things in her life: a restaurant manager, a clinical research coordinator, a dreamer, a makeup brand ambassador, an event coordinator, a blogger, and more. But at heart, she's always been a writer, and in 2020 she decided to make it official. Good luck stopping her now.

ALSO BY HANNAH MCBRIDE

Blackwater Pack Series:

SANCTUM

BROKEN

PREY

LEGACY

SCARS (coming Winter 2022)

For giveaways, teasers, and overall fangirling about books, join the Facebook Group:

BLACKWATER PACK

Mad World Series:

MAD WORLD (coming Fall 2021)

Printed in Great Britain
by Amazon